Formation of Planet

Pero Metkovic

authorHOUSE®

AuthorHouse™
1663 Liberty Drive, Suite 200
Bloomington, IN 47403
www.authorhouse.com
Phone: 1-800-839-8640

First published by AuthorHouse 2/24/2009

ISBN: 978-1-4389-5739-5 (sc)
ISBN: 978-1-4389-5740-1 (e)

Printed in the United States of America
Bloomington, Indiana

This book is printed on acid-free paper.

FORMATION OF BODY

In old Babylon, 2 300 years BC, Earth has been explained as a firm ground surrounded by a salty river, what meant the sea. The theory of Earth being the center of universe came later. Ptolemy has accepted this theory. The theory was spread out and worth for centuries.

Copernicus in 1,543 year found Heliocentric System. He created the system that has been worth till nowadays. Earth and the planets are circling around the Sun which is the central body.

Is this theory exact? Way would the planets circle around the Sun? For any motion in celestial space a power should be needed!

The Sun does not possess any power, which would force the other planets to circle around it. It does not create any physical influence to them. Any energy that could be produced by the Sun cannot influence other planets to move. The reason is large distance of planets from the Sun, and other physical circumstances. Accordingly there is not a realistic ground that the planets have to circle around the Sun, which is the central body of the Solar System.

The Sun is fixed body, which is totally, or partly still one. It means the Sun is the body that does not move in celestial space. If it moves, than its speed is neglect. The Sun maybe still follows its path of emerge. Such path was created by a power that pushed the body into the space, out of a base body. The Sun maybe still easily rotates around its axis.

All bodies in the Solar System emerged from one large, or initial, base body. A base body disintegrated and created a group of new planets. There were a few possibilities how a base body disintegrated. It could happen by explosion, eruption, or collision with another planet.

A lot of newly erupted hot liquid mass emerged into celestial space. The mass transformed into new bodies, or planets. Newly emerged masses cooled down in celestial space. They became solid or partly solid bodies. All of them were of different masses, but same composition. Some were very small of a few meters diameter, and another ones enormous large. So are existing planets now. Some has very small masses, and another are enormous large.

A newly emerged planets were launched into celestial space on their paths of emerge. New paths were usually curves of different appearances, or straight lines. Planets reached different ranges by their speed of emerge. Even if planets are hovering now, they may still be moving by their initial speeds. Besides that, they may still be following their initial paths.

We can compare the Sun to the other bodies of the Solar System. The Sun may still be in possession of its speed of emerge, that keeps it moving on its initial path. It means that the Sun is actually similar to the other planets.

All other bodies of the Solar System are equal. Planets are partly, or totally still bodies. They are hovering in celestial space. Most probably some of them are still moving on their paths of emerge by neglect speeds. Some bodies are still rotating round their axis, while others are totally still ones. One of such rotating bodies is our Earth.

This theory opens a new idea of "Relatively Fixed Bodies" in the Solar System. All bodies of the Solar System could be considered as relatively fixed or still ones. The idea is similar to all other celestial bodies wherever they are in celestial space. They are totally still hovering masses, or they move on their paths of emerge throughout the space.

In celestial space we may encounter very low temperatures that are lower than absolute zero. These temperatures we can call Mega Zero, as they are not measurable for us. We cannot reach such temperatures with techniques, and knowledge, that we have today. Besides we have not such instruments that could measure these temperatures. We can expect Mega zero temperatures in celestial space that are not very far from Earth.

A body that hovers in celestial space has been cooled down for thousands of centuries. The original hot liquid mass of a body has been surrounded by a coldness of the space that has influenced it. In such circumstances a body mass has been transformed from its liquid to a solid composition.

The bodies in celestial space are partly or totally cooled down. Some of them are firm, solid masses. Other ones possess glow, liquid interiors, that is wrapped by a firm cover.

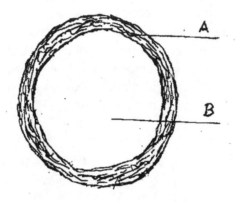

A - Solid layer. B – Internal liquid mass.

Body on the sketch is partially cooled with developed surface layer. Its interior is composed of a liquid, glow mass.

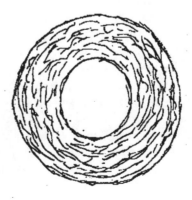

Partially cooled body with a well developed surface layer and certain quantity of a liquid, glow mass in its interior.

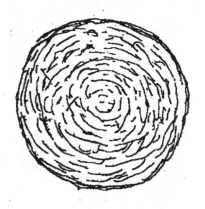

Entire cooled planet. Its whole structure is solid.

Certain groups of new bodies in celestial space have emerged by disintegration of a larger planet, or by collision of two bodies. A new group of bodies that emerged can be located into particular segment of a volume.

Various groups of bodies compose different forms at celestial sphere. We, from Earth can hardly define their real shapes, but anyhow we can sort them in certain configurations, called constellations. It means that these groups are mostly defined as we can see them, what is not in accordance to their realistic shapes. They may look like a particular figure, but their real arrangement in celestial space is unknown to us. It means that bodies can be very distant each from other, but we can still see them, being a certain figure on celestial sphere. A figure that we can see on firmament is only projection of real celestial bodies.

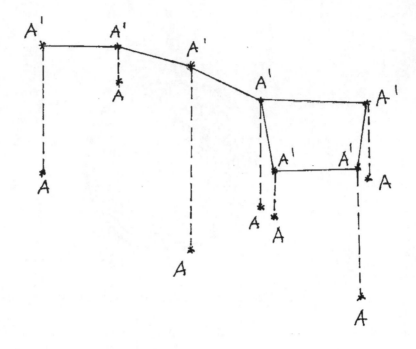

A. Real position of a celestial body. A'. Projected position of a celestial body.

On the sketch above we can see a group of stars that form particular constellation. A figure that we see on celestial sphere is marked by stars A'. Such points are actually projections of stars on celestial sphere. Their real positions are in points A.

Any constellation that we can see on celestial sphere shows only projected stars. Their real positions we cannot define. All those figures that have particular names are only grouped according to our visual effect. Stars can be far away one from other, or in any direction. On celestial sphere their projections will show particular figure that we can name as Ursa Major, for example.

Stretch of a planet in voluminous shape. Celestial bodies spread to all sides in the space.

It means that celestial bodies have stretched from the main body, as a center, to maximum distances they have reached. We can say that all these bodies have emerged from one common base body that has erupted. Now a base body is still central body of this group of planets.

Spiral eruptions. Newly emerged bodies lie in a plane superficies.

Rotating planet erupts its mass spirally. It means an accumulation of new bodies make spiral form in celestial space. All bodies lie in a plane superficies. Newly emerged system seems flat to us. System is not deep as voluminous one. Similarity can be seen in eruption of Spiral Nebula in constellation Canes Venetici.

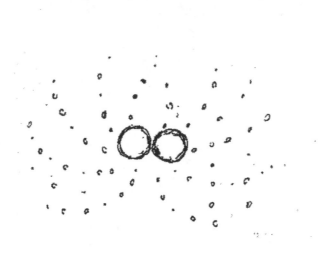

Figurative eruptions caused by collision of two planets.

Two celestial bodies collided. A stretch of their masses is irregular. Elements of newly developed masses are stretching out in different ways. Newly emerged masses have become from both bodies that collided. A hot, liquid mass will transfer into newly emerged bodies. Actually bodies of this group of planets will emerge from an existing liquid mass.

Spiral Nebula in constellation Canes Venetici.

The photo shows Spiral Nebula in constellation Canes Venetici. Nebula of a spiral form can be seen at the photo, and another spherical body in its vicinity. Here, a collision of two bodies is obvious. Remaining mass of Spiral Nebula is rotating around its center. The body is stretching out its mass that will create new bodies in its surroundings. Spherical body situated in the vicinity of Nebula is a still one.

If celestial body explodes, like Spiral Nebula, a stretch of its mass will be visible to us, even its smaller parts. Later such mass will be transformed into planets, and other smaller celestial bodies, that will be cooling down in the space. Now nearly the entire mass of Nebula stretch is visible to us. Later when planets become formed, we shall hardly be able to recognize some of them. Entire mass will convert into smaller cooled bodies that will not show any more in celestial sphere.

At the photo of Spiral Nebula central mass of the body is the most visible and most compact one. Another spiral mass is stretching out from central part of the body. It means that the body looses its mass in the space. Such mass will be converted into thousands of bodies of various sizes, like planets, asteroids, or even smaller ones.

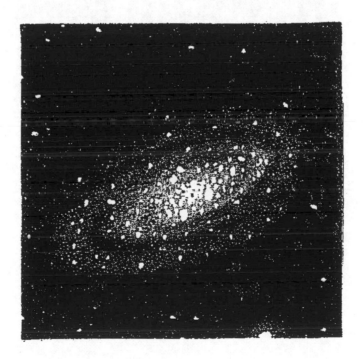

Spiral formation of mass scattered from an erupted base body.

The mass of a base body is still rotating. The glow, liquid mass is following way of rotation. It will cool down in celestial space, and transform into new bodies.

View of celestial sphere in the night. Light spots show newly born systems.

A loose of gravity can be reason of explosion of a celestial body. A body will explode at the moment of a lose of gravity, if its interior content is liquid. The force of gravity holds particles of a body assembled in one mutual composition. When a body loses its force of gravity, it will disintegrate.

Such celestial body we can call a soft one. It means that the body has not developed solid cover, or a skin. Its interior consists of a liquid glow mass for a very big percent of a planet. We can divide volume of a planet into graduation. This way we can find out how much certain body is soft, or solid.

Entire solid bodies have not any liquid, glow mass in their interiors. They consist of one piece of a solid matter. They will not disintegrate if they lose gravity. Their mass will remain solid and compact. On the other hand if soft body loses gravity, it will easily disintegrate and discharge its liquid interior into the space.

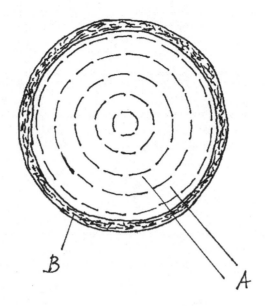

A. Grades of a liquid glow mass in interior of a celestial body. B. Solid wrap that surrounds liquid, glow mass of a body.

On the sketch above a celestial body is covered by a solid wrap that surrounds its liquid, glow interior. A planet is soft, as thickness of its wrap is only round 10 percent of the entire body. In case of lose of gravity such body will easily explode, and discharge its liquid mass.

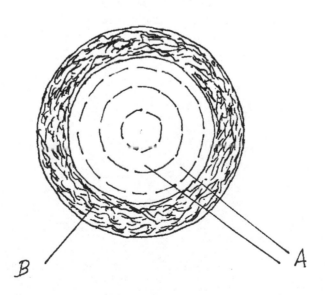

A. Grades of liquid glow mass in interior of a body. B. Solid wrap.

On the sketch above it can be seen a celestial body that has well developed solid wrap. A wrap takes about 30 percent of a planet. A planet is not soft any more, neither entire solid. If such body loses gravity, it may explode, and discharge its liquid interior into the space.

Gravity is a component of rotation. On the other hand rotation and gravity are components of launching force of emerge of a body. Throughout time periods, a body has been losing base launching force. In the end it will loose rotation and gravity. If a body possesses liquid, glow interior, it will disintegrate. A glow liquid mass will erupt into celestial space. The mass will rotate and cool down throughout immense periods of time. In the end such mass will create new bodies of different sizes.

Only large planets possess liquid, glow mass in their interiors. It depends on dimension of a body, whether it will have solid or liquid interior. Small bodies, like meteors are cooling down much faster and they are mainly solid. Planets of large dimensions remain glow, liquid mass, covered by a solid skin.

A glow, liquid mass that erupts from a disintegrated body will confront coldness of celestial space. A mass will move throughout celestial space pushed by its launch energy. It will not reach much further from its base body, what can be seen on the photos of erupted bodies. Finally a mass will convert into separated parts that will commence to rotate. New celestial bodies of various sizes will emerge from a mass.

Rotating, glow mass is surrounded by a coldness of celestial space. A mass is future planet that is still developing its skin. A liquid mass at the brim of a future planet is becoming solid under strong influence of celestial coldness. A planet is still soft, having only light skin over its surface. In long periods of time, a planet will be developing its solid skin. Bodies of smaller sizes will become solid sooner, than large ones.

Individual groups of bodies in celestial space have become by breakup of a base larger body, or by collision of two bodies. New group of bodies that emerged in the space can be located in a particular segment of volume. It is new product of an explosion, that occurred somewhere in the firmament.

It is obvious that mainly new emerged planets are stretching to all sides of their based body. It also depends on a shape of eruption that can be volumetric, or spiral. Spiral eruptions are mainly flat, and newly emerged bodies spread in a flat surface of celestial space.

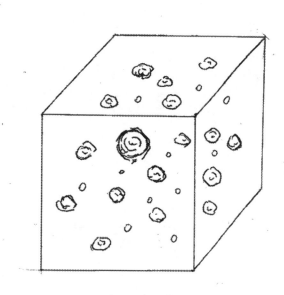

Volumetric stretch of newly emerged celestial bodies. They move away from an initial body that has exploded.

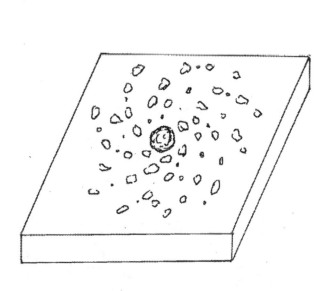

Spiral stretch of planets. Celestial bodies detached from a base body in a spiral shape. The stretch of planets is not voluminous, but flat one.

Planets that possess liquid interior, in an event of explosion create new bodies. We can say that such planets are reproductive. They are creating new bodies in celestial space. If a body is whole cooled, or solid, it is not reproductive. Liquid, glow magma is only reproductive matter in celestial space.

The celestial bodies are at different degree of cool down. Some of them are entire solid, besides others that are liquid and wrapped by a solid envelope. Soon after an explosion of a particular body, entire new liquid groups of masses emerge. Masses will cool down and remain in celestial space.

Earth is only a small part of a base mass that could be attributed to Earth. Earth has been separated from a mutual base body mass. All the rest of a mass, that has been separated as Earth has scattered into celestial space. This means that one part of mutual glow liquid mass has become separate unit, being Earth. Other parts of a mass have separated as the Sun, than planets, and so on.

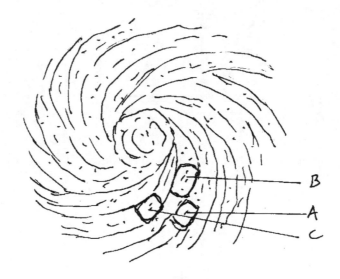

Division of a mutual glow, liquid mass emerged from a base body.
A. Earth B. The Sun C. Mars

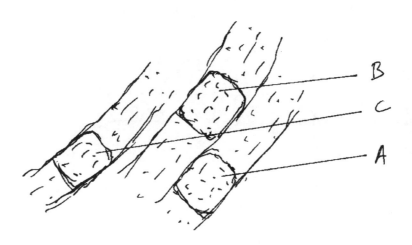

Realistic masses of newly emerged celestial bodies.
A. Earth B. The Sun C. Mars

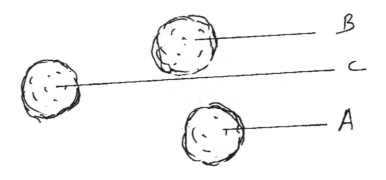

Planets that emerged from initial glow liquid mass are already formed.
A. Earth B. The Sun C. Mars

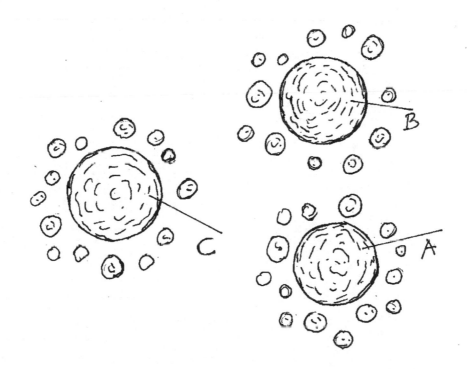

Formed planets that emerged from mutual liquid glow mass. They are surrounded with celestial bodies that emerged from a mutual mass.

A. Earth B. The Sun C. Mars

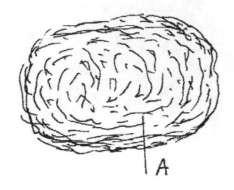

Separated mass of Earth emerged from a mutual based body.
A. Total mass of Earth B. Real mass of Earth

From a base mass that has belonged to Earth many smaller bodies of different sizes have emerged. They are surrounding Earth, being invisible to us. Some of these bodies are meteors that we can see in the night, when they enter in our atmosphere.

A large part of a base mass, maybe even more than 70 % that has belonged to Earth has scattered in celestial space. Such mass has been converted into bodies of different sizes up to very small ones. Bodies are hovering in the space on different distances from Earth. Most of them do not posses any energy that could be emitted in the space.

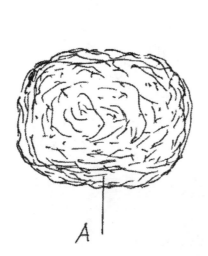
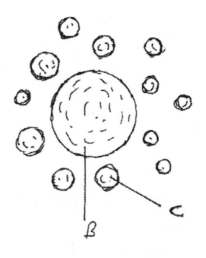

A. Erupted mass which Earth became from. B. Real mass of a formed planet Earth. C. Celestial bodies in vicinity of Earth that emerged from a same initial mass.

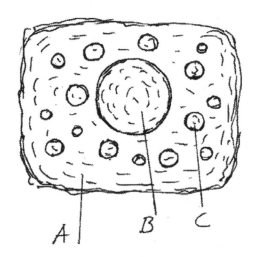

Comparison of a mutual liquid, glow mass that Earth emerged from, with surrounding bodies that emerged from a same mass.
A. Volume of a liquid, glow mass. B. Earth C. Surrounding body.

Appearance of Super Nova indicates an emerge of new bodies in celestial space. A reason can be explosion, or collision of two bodies. A great amount of liquid mass releases in the space that will convert into newly formed bodies of different dimensions. Mainly smaller bodies surround main planet, even if they can be of larger dimension for us.

All celestial bodies have same structure. Diversity is only in degree of cooling. All of them are spherical structures, built from a liquid magma that has cooled down. Many bodies have a glow, liquid mass in their interiors that is wrapped by a solid envelope. Gravity of a body, and solid wrap hold liquid interior assembled in a structure of celestial body.

Gas stars do not exist in celestial space, but only liquid and solid masses. We cannot see any mass in space, if it does not emit energy. Gas has no potentency to emit energy that can be visible from Earth. A gas in space, free of body's gravity, deals and disappears in forms of endless petty elements. We can compare a gas with Earth's atmosphere, being of similar composition as the air.

Earth atmosphere being composed of the air wraps the sphere. The force of gravity holds the atmosphere in immediate vicinity to Earth. Otherwise the air of the atmosphere would disappear in the space, as Earth is progressively moving ahead. The air would hover in the space as a cloud, having its particles in vicinity each to other. The particles would deal into endless tiny parts, as there would not be any force to keep them gathered.

The air or a gas in the space is exposed to coldness. We can imagine confront of a gas that sets free from liquid, glow magma, and a coldness of the space. Magma will smelt being converted into a solid matter. If a gas being composed into a structure of a liquid, glow magma erupts into the space, it will cool down.

In the end of the atmosphere the air mass is very cold, even less than absolute zero. Particles of a gas in the space are cold and minimized. Any matter exposed to coldness will squeeze, otherwise if exposed to heat, it w0uld spread out.

Actually from our point of knowledge we can hardly define a state of the gas in celestial space. We can only compare it with its state on Earth, where the gas is under influence of gravity. Besides in the space the gas is exposed to a very low temperature of mega zero that we cannot measure on Earth.

Only solid bodies that have a glow, liquid interior, and glow surface can emit energy. Emission of energy spreads from bodies throughout celestial space, and it reaches far distances. The larger the body is, if it has a glow, liquid interior, it will emit stronger energy. Their energy will reach longer distances, then energy of smaller bodies.

New liquid mass emerges in celestial space by explosion of a planet. A mass is moving in the space by its launching energy. Elements of a mass are of various sizes. Some are large volumes ones, while others are entire tiny. They will convert into celestial bodies, after cooling process.

Celestial bodies move in celestial space on their paths of emerge. Their distances from initial planet depend of a launching speed. Any particular body will stop at a point of range. It means a newly formed planet will reach its final point, where it will lose launching energy. A planet will stop, and it will hover in celestial space.

Herewith it could be implemented a new theory of range, or reach. It says that any body launched in celestial space will reach its final point of range. If body is launched by a power of explosion into celestial space, it will move until a moment when it will lose the launching energy. We can say that the body has reached its point of range. The body will rotate until a moment when it will lose a whole energy. Finally the body will hover in its position of range in celestial space.

A path of mass element can be straight, or parabolic, dependently on conditions of launching. A path depends how Nova explodes, and launches its parts in celestial space. Newly formed planets will have different paths, as strait, parabolic, or any other appearance. If explosion of body is volumetric, than newly emerged planets will move in the space on their strait paths. Spiral eruptions will launch glow mass in spiral, or parabolic paths.

Newly formed bodies when moving in celestial space are losing energy. They begin to rotate around own axis, due to their improper forms. Newly became rotation is a component of their launching force. It means that launching energy of a planet transforms in rotating energy. The body will commence to rotate round its axis, and become spherical. A reason is a transformation of its launching into rotating energy.

The body assumes spherical shape, as a liquid structure of mass' elements is suitable for molding. Axis of rotation are changeable in temporal periods. Form of the body becomes more and more spherical, or round. It means that during the periods of time, the body will be changing its axis of rotation, becoming more and more spherically shaped.

All bodies in celestial space have assumed a spherical form, even if they have emerged from volumetric, irregular structure of a liquid, glow mass. The reason is rotation and gravity that will transform initial mass into spherical form of the body. This is a main low of rotation that says the body will assume spherical shape, if influenced by rotation, and gravity in celestial space.

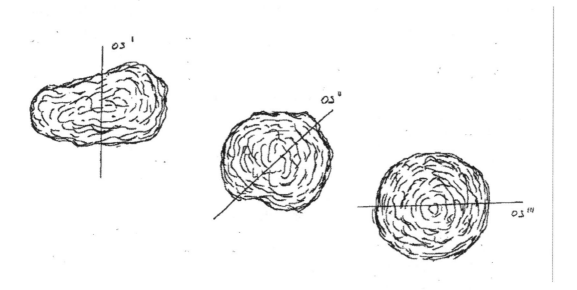

On the sketch, a transformation of an improper form of mass' element into a sphere can be seen
(OS = Axis).

A body passes phases of transformation from an improper to a spherical form. It is
cooling and adopting a solid surface layer. An element of mass has become a sphere, owing to a
plastic glow matter, that has been treated in immense periods of time. Permanent change of axis
of rotation throughout a time has formed its final shape of a sphere.

All celestial bodies that are visible to us are spheres. The Sun, the Moon, and the planets
have a spherical form. If we compare them with Earth, than logically it should be a sphere.
Today's science considers Earth as ellipsoid, what is not acceptable. Definitely it is a sphere, as
any other celestial body in the firmament. Earth being a sphere has a different volume of one that
was calculated for ellipsoid. It means that Earth has more volume than it is presently known.

The science says that the Sun has not a surface solid layer like other planets. It says that it
is entire liquid, glow body. However the Sun also has solid cover, same as all other celestial
bodies. Its internal glow mass emits large quantities of energy that reaches us on Earth.

The planets of Solar system are partly cooled bodies. They emit certain quantity of
energy of light. The Moon also emits energy of light. The Moon is not enlightened by Sun's light,
how the science says. Energy of the Moon is weak, but still we can see it, as it is most probably
situated nearby Earth.

We cannot see many bodies in celestial space. Some of them are entire cooled, or they
emit weak energy of light. Besides, some celestial bodies are very distant from us. Even if they
emit strong energy, we cannot see them, as their energy cannot reach us. Dimensions of some
bodies can be large, like dimensions of existing planets. They can be situated in our vicinity, but
still we shall not see them. The power of energy of light, and distance from us are factors, that we
can notice certain body in the space.

Visibility of a planet depends on glow, liquid mass in its interior that emits energy.
Partially, or nearly entire cooled bodies emit a weak energy of light. Quantity of emitting energy
depends on size of surface layer of celestial body. It means, if the body has developed a solid
surface layer, it will emit weaker energy. Again, all depends, how large the body is, and how big
quantity of a glow, liquid mass it possess in its interior.

Black Holes could be considered as bodies, that emits a weak energy of light. There are
several of them in Solar System. They are visible to us, because they still emit a weak energy that
we can discern in celestial space.

Distant bodies are hardly visible from Earth. Even thaw we see them, and we can say that they emit energy. They are maybe relatively powerful sources of energy. However due to far distance from Earth they are hardly noticeable.

Gas Stars, actually joints of gas in celestial space, even if they exist, cannot be visible from Earth, as they do not emit any energy of light. They could be explained as zones of gas, actually as very tiny parcels of dispersed gas that remained after explosion of the body. Dealing of particles is enormous large, and such gas cannot be identified as a matter any more. A gas diminishes into so tiny elements, and very long distances between its particles.

Here are short explanations of theories that will be met in further text of the book. It is necessary to acquaint with theory of particles in view to understand some parts of the following. Theory says that any matter on earth, or in celestial space is composed of particles, which are only a notion. The particles are minimizing to the endless small. They are positioned on certain distances one to another. There is a vacuum field in the space between particles. Solid bodies have dense composition of particles with minimized distance between them. Contrary, particles of gas are very distant one to another. There is much more of vacuum space between them, than at ones of solid bodies. Between solid matters, as metals, stone etc, there are varieties of structures that are less solid or soft. Liquids, like water, oils etc. are less solid then metals, but more solid then gases.

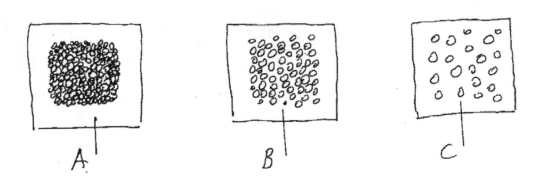

Various compositions of particles of different matters, what depends how solid they are.
A. Particles of very solid matters like metals, stones etc. B. Particles of average solid matters, like water and other liquids. C. Particles of matters that are not solid, like air and gases.

Theory of particles differs from molecular theory. It says that particles are only a notion, but they are actually not. Any matter in the nature is real and existing, no matter how solid, or soft it is. Therefore, particles are real and existing. How small they are, we cannot say. That's way we call them only a notion, as we cannot imagine their volumes.

Particles of matters of same composition are kept together, being formed in a same form. Still particles have possessed some power of their previous energy, as it has not completely vanished. Previously the matter has been a liquid glow mass. Later it has cooled in a certain form. Particles still possess part of a static energy from their previous state. It means that particles are still not ideally cooled and still. They have a tendency of scattering and expel one from another. Remaining of their energy is minimal and neglected. They will remain composed in an existing form.

Particles of any liquid, glow mass possess energy. They are explosive, being hot and glow, having a tendency to react and explode. If we heat any matter, its particles will become reactive. Opposite, if we cool down a matter, its particles will become still ones, and they will lose energy.

Actually, if we heat any matter, it will absorb energy of heat. Its particles will become reactive, and explosive. The whole matter has tendency to spread out, and become larger. It means that particles are bombing one – another, making whole matter explosive. Opposite, if we cool down a matter, it has tendency to squeeze down, or to become smaller. The particles are losing energy, and they are becoming still ones.

This idea leads us to a composition of particles. Final tiny material part of particle is gassy one. That is a part that we could not imagine previously, and we called it only a notion. Any matter on Earth, or in celestial space is composed of gas, no matter, how solid it is. Final tiny parts of its particles are gassy ones. Even very solid matters, as diamonds, metals etc, are composed of gassy particles.

Liquid, glow magma that is the main structure of any celestial body is composed of particles. Their final tiny elements are gassy ones. If the liquid, glow magma cools down, it will produce different matters, as minerals, stones, oils, water, air etc. Final tiny elements of their particles are gassy ones.

It is the best to perceive composition of the air to understand structure of particles. The air is composed of particles like any other matter. Distances between particles of the air are acceptable for us. It is easier to understand them, then ones of a solid matter, even if they exist there. The space between particles is a vacuum.

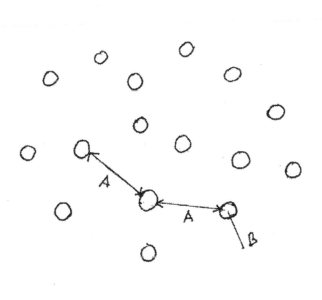

Particles of the air. They are situated on certain distances one to another.
A. Distances. B. Particles

Even biological matter is composed of particles. They are made of different state then of minerals, or other structures of unlived matter. Human beings possess bones, flesh and other compositions of their bodies. Particles of each part of a human body are composed differently. Same is with zoological and biological world.

Following examples show that any matter on Earth, or in celestial space is composed of the gas. If a piece of iron stays at sea bottom for long, it will disappear. Sometimes we can see an iron peace on sea bottom. If we take it in our hands, we shall notice that only a small part of previous mass remained. We shall have only peaces of corrosion in our hands. Sea water and corrosion transformed a piece of iron into a gas.

A. An iron bar that corroded at sea bottom. B. Peaces of corrosion remain from a bar. Nearly whole iron bar disappeared. Only small parts of corrosions remained.

Sometimes in a forest we can see dry wooden branch lying on a ground. If we take it in our hands, it will break in peaces. We shall ascertain that only a small part of previous mass remained. We can collect it like small wooden peaces. Due to corrosion of rain and humidity, all the rest disappeared as a gas.

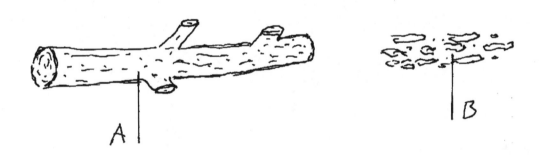

A. Wooden branch. B. Remaining of a wooden branch.
Very small quantity of wooden peaces remained from a rotten branch.

Even a stone, found in the nature can break into small peaces in our hands. Composition of such stone is much softer than of other ones. Rain and climate circumstances converted that stone into a gas. We shall have only sand, and small pieces of stone in our hands. We can crumble nearly a whole such stone in our hands.

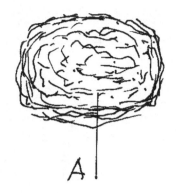

Stone corroded by rain. B. A handful quantity of sand remained after a stone. Whole stone converted into sand under influence of weather.

We can conclude that in all these cases, a great part of volumes of mentioned objects have disappeared. Only small remaining can be identified as corrosion, sand or wooden peaces. A great part of previous mass volume converted into a gas. All matters on Earth, like stones, soil etc., transform into a gas under influence of weather. The stones become holed, and smaller due to rain falls.

All these matters of unlived world have become from a glow, liquid mass that has cooled under different conditions. They have been pressed into different forms in the nature. Dependently on a pressure, and kind of form, matters of different firmness have emerged. Their base mass was mutual liquid, glow magma. Therefore, in the nature we have matters of different firmness, even if they belong to the same kind. Stones can be solid, and firm, or even very soft, and we can easily crumble them in our hands.

Celestial space is endless and airless. Bodies are hovering in it, or they are moving by their launch energy. There is not any resistance in the space that could influence energy of bodies. Bodies are moving by their speed of emerge, which is leading them to approaching points of a range.

Any celestial body will reach its point of a range, which depends on its launching power. A body will become fixed or still one. It will rotate around its own axis for sometimes, until it totally loses energy. Entire solid masses, without liquid internal structure, that reach point of range are hovering bodies. They do not rotate any more, or posses any gravity.

Observing supernova we can notice that masses of newly formed bodies reach only certain range from a base body. Mass' elements in vicinity of center are more condensed, that once situated at a brim. Those bodies will remain forever in vicinity of a base body. They will occupy that particular part of the space.

A proof of arise of new bodies in celestial space are nova and supernova. We can notice increased light around a group of newly raised bodies. They will become new solid masses in celestial space.

We can see only a part of celestial space filled by celestial bodies. The rest of the space is deep, and for our opinion endless. It means that our science has not yet reached those far zones of firmament. The word endless actually means something that we have not yet discovered.

Existing section of celestial space that we know is filled by bodies. We can say that bodies emerge by division. The base body explodes, and it divides into another smaller ones.

The Solar System is a segment of the space, where bodies of the same origin exist. We can bring a theory of mutual origin of bodies in celestial space. A theory basis is that they emerged by an explosion of mutual body of a larger mass. An explosion has caused disperse, and rise of new bodies, relatively of a new celestial system. This means that all bodies in celestial space could be of a same origin. A composition of their masses has become from liquid, glow magma.

Suppose that celestial solid matter has become from same larger body, which split into smaller ones. Newly emerged bodies have again split further on. It is a process of disintegration of a larger, and formation of new smaller bodies.

Let's imagine that the based body has existed somewhere in a center of today's star system. All solid bodies have become out of it. At first it has exploded, and created new smaller bodies. Bodies have passed rotation processes forming spherical shape, and other characters of a solid matter.

Newly formed bodies are losing gravity. They have exploded again causing formations of new smaller bodies. Process is in principle endless until tiny bodies completely grow solid and they lose liquid masses in their interiors.

Particular sphere can encircle segment of space where all celestial bodies are situated. The rest is free and unidentified space for us. That part of celestial space we can call endless.

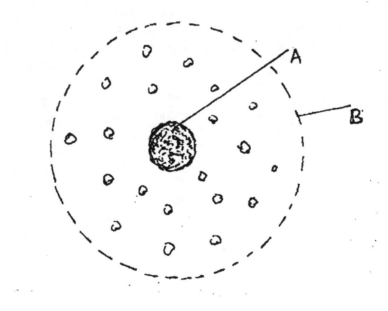

A- Supposed initial body, which from has emerged disperse of a liquid, glow mass.
B- Brim of a sphere.

At the picture it can be seen a sphere as segment of the space, where bodies of same origin are situated. All around the sphere is for us unknown, endless space. This part of the space we can understand like something in connection one to another, solid masses and airless space. It means that in certain segment of celestial space we can identify solid bodies that are hovering in it. That fact leads us to understand unity of airless space, and solid bodies in such segment. Otherwise celestial space is immense, and endless for our knowledge.

Anything in celestial space that is far, and not investigated by us we can call endless. We know Solar System, and some another parts of celestial sphere. These parts are somehow understandable for us and we shall not call them endless. Those areas of celestial space that are not learned by us, we can call immense and endless zones.

Solar System is a part of the space that we can understand much easier than other ones. We can imagine airless space with celestial bodies that hover in it. We can identify bodies like Earth, the Sun, and Mars etc that are situated in a certain space. Here, is mutual unity of airless space understandable and celestial bodies situated in such space.

We can imagine that somewhere in a center of the space filled by celestial bodies still exists rests of initial large mass. The most probably it has dispersed only partially. When supernova forms, large part of a mass remains compact, while only some part disperses into the space, let's say 20 to 50%.

Today's view of planet structure is a break out of magma from Earth's interior. Regarding composition, Earth could be similar to all celestial bodies. Structure of magma will change by cooling into various forms, dependently of temperatures and pressure. Minerals, stones and many other forms will arise from a glow, liquid magma.

GRAVITY

During emerge of a body, launching energy created rotation, being its component. Force of Gravity is newly raised product of rotation. All bodies in celestial space strive for rotation. Reason is immaterial space, without any resistance. Launching energy of celestial body transforms into rotating force.

Gravity acts to the center of rotating body. Vectors are semicircle, and curled to the center. Gravity holds a liquid mass assembled. It detains disappear of a mass of body. Gravity attracts gaseous evaporations to Earth. Particles of gases do not vanish into celestial space being attracted by gravity. Gravity attracts all matters equally, regardless of composition. We can say that gravity acts like a force of wind.

In the other words, vectors of gravity force are sucking any matter in direction of Earth's center. No matter what kind of a matter it is, it will be sucked by gravity. Actually gravity is producing vacuum in the air mass of atmosphere. It is attracting particles of the air, and of any other matter in direction of Earth's center.

Vectors of gravity are curled, or parabolic in direction of Earth's center. Such shapes of vectors are created by rotation of Earth. It means that they are making certain whirlwind around center of Earth.

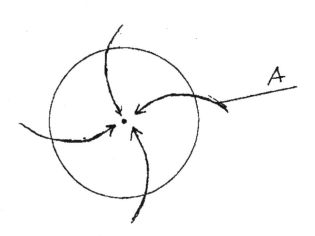

A- Curved vectors of gravity
Appearance of gravity of a rotating body.

Gravity has formed spherical shapes of all celestial bodies, while their mass was inflamed and liquid. Earth is still plastic, as its interior is liquid and suitable for shaping.

Rotation of Earth can be observed through centripetal and centrifugal forces. One acts to a center and other to a brim of a body. Gravity is a product of centripetal force, what means that the body is rotating so, that force acts to a center. It means that Earth has been forced to rotate from its brim.

Launching energy emerged at a moment of explosion of the prime body. It transformed into rotating force that acted to a brim of sphere. New product of rotating force is gravity.

24

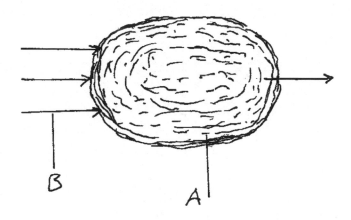

A. Celestial body pushed in space. B. Launching energy.
Body transits celestial space pushed by launching energy.

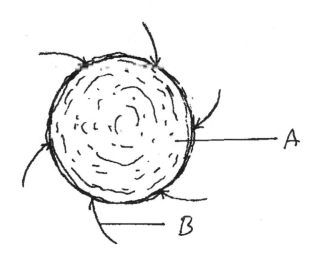

A. Body commences rotating. B. Launching energy transforms into rotating force
Launching energy that transforms into rotating force acts from a brim of body.

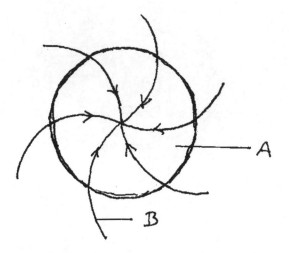

A. Body at rotating phase. B. Vectors of gravity.
Rotating force transforms into gravity. Vectors act from a brim of a body in direction of center.

If we want to explain gravity, we shall take stick and cord. In the end of cord we can hang small weight. We shall see that during rotation cord will wind around stick. Vectors of gravity can be compared to the cord. It means that Gravity will attract any matter to Earth's center.

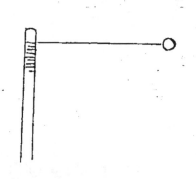

Stick with cord and weight. When rotating cord winds around stick.

In cyclone wind turns around center. The wind is forming whirly stream. This is also an example of act of force from a brim to center.

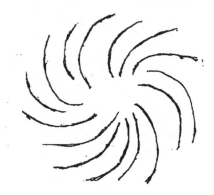

Winding of the air mass to a center in the cyclone.

If we rotate glassy ball, a sand inside will collect around axe of rotation. This is another example of rotating force that acts to center.

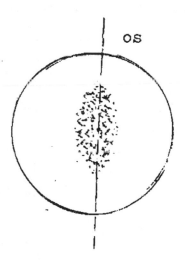

Glassy ball with a send inside.
Glassy ball rotates. Send assembles round central axis.

These examples can affirm that gravity is a vector of Earth's rotation. Gravity acts like a wave on matters of different structures. Effects will be various, dependently of structure of matter, and relatively of its specific gravity.

Weight of a body is vector of gravity, in other words effect of gravity on dimension of matter. Heavy masses are attracted faster by gravity to surface of a planet than light ones.

Disposition of gases occurs in the atmosphere. Heavier gases are closer to Earth's surface, than lighter ones that rise up to higher layers of atmosphere. This is also act of gravity that disposes gases to the different layers of the atmosphere, according to their specific gravities.

The similar process occurs with liquids. Warmer water in the nature rises up, above colder one. This way disposition of specific gravities of matters is carried out under influence of Earth's gravity.

Effect of gravity is resultant of a force. Vectors divert to a center of a mass. It could be slight difference in strength of gravity between north, and south poles to equator. Gravity could be the strongest at zones of equator, but to the poles it diminishes.

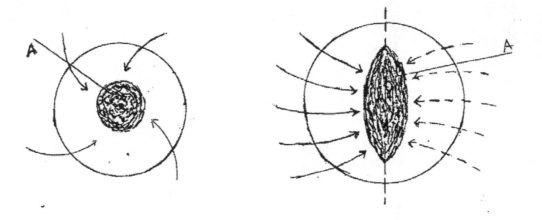

A. Imagined body of concentration of gravity effect.

Resultant effect of vectors of gravity manifests in concentration of gravity. It can be illustrated by a shape of imagined body in Earth interior. The curves of gravity bend to a center of imagined body. They form whirl pool of vectors of gravity force round the center of Earth. In the center of Earth the force of gravity is the strongest.

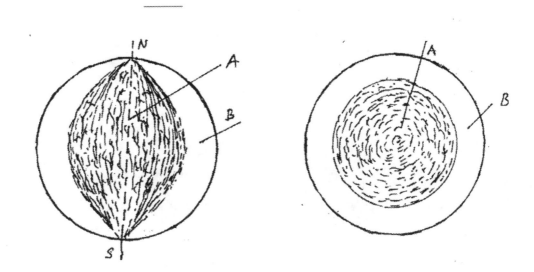

A- Interior imagined body of stronger gravity force zone.
B- Zone of weaker force of gravity.

Force of gravity acts variously from poles to equator. Earth can be divided in polar zone of the force, middle latitudes, and equatorial zone.

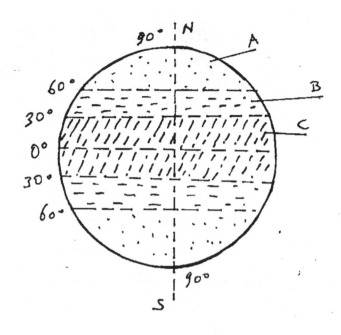

A- Polar zone. B – Middle latitudes. C – Equatorial zone.
Variety of gravity force.

Force of gravity weakens in celestial space at longer distances from Earth surface. On its limitation line force is totally weak. Space from Earth surface to limitation of gravity effect can be divided into grades of efficiency.

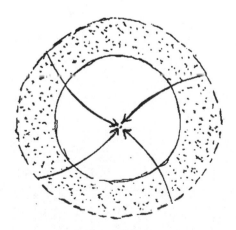

Field of gravity effect with limitation line

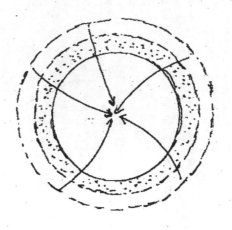

Grades of gravity effect.

Force of gravity is the strongest in a center of rotating body. It is weaker on Earth's surface. Rising higher into Earth's atmosphere, gravity becomes weaker and weaker.

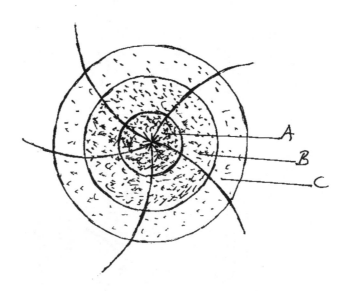

Grades of strength of gravity in Earth interior.
A. Central area, where gravity is the strongest B. Area of average strength of gravity. C. Area of the lowest strength of gravity.

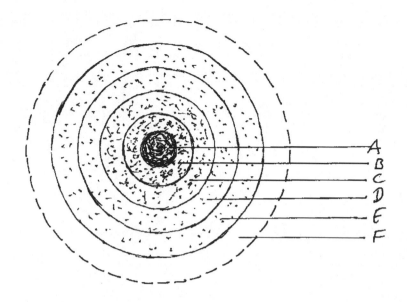

Division of strength of gravity. A. The area of the strongest force of gravity. B, C, D Strength of gravity diminishes with a distance from center of Earth. E. Force of gravity at Earth's surface layer. F. Strength of gravity in atmosphere.

Suppose that we could be able to build the channel throughout Earth mass. We could than throw a metal ball throughout it. The ball would fall down until the center of Earth. It would receive force of inertia that is caused by gravity. The ball may fall lower than the center of Earth, for a value of inertia, what is questionable. Than it would come back and hover in the center of Earth, actually in the strongest field of gravity.

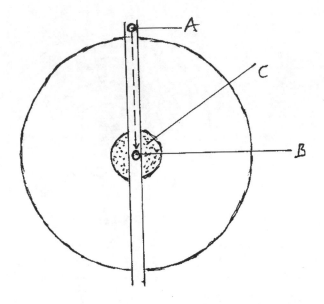

A. Metal ball that has been thrown into a channel, that leads throughout the center of Earth. B. Final position of a metal ball. C. An area of the strongest force of gravity

A degree of gravity effect with distance from Earth's surface is hard to assume. We can say that gravity has an effect to approximately 1/3 of Earth's diameter or more. This is taken as hypothesis for better understanding of gravity.

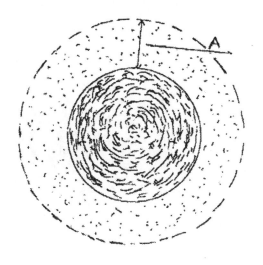

A – 1/3 of diameter of planet or more.
Field of Gravity.

Efficiency of gravity force is resultant. Vectors divert to a center of body. There could be slight difference of gravity effect from north, and south to equator.

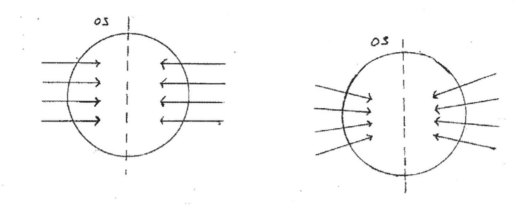

Liner vectors of gravity converge. Resultant effect is to a
center of sphere (OS = Axis).

This way a system for measuring of Earth gravity could be established. The instrument could be made, similar to one that is measuring atmospheric pressure. A value of one gravity unit could be taken as standard. Such unit would be manifested by change of mercury scale in a glass vessel. Instrument should be insolated from influence of weather changes. This way the strength of Earth's field could be measured.

The instrument should consist of glassy tube with graduation. It should be positioned under a vacuum glassy cover in order to minimize influence of weather changes. In any case changes of atmospheric pressure would influence instrument and produce error in a value of measured gravity.

Atmospheric and submerged pressures are actually parameters of gravity force. Pillar of the air on Earth surface is defined by weight of it on square centimeter. Such pillar shows strength of gravity to the unit of one centimeter. The pillar under water could be defined by weight of the water on the square centimeter of bottom, what depends on a depth of the water.

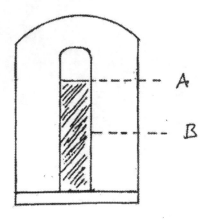

A – One gravity unit. B – 0.5 of gravity unit.
An instrument for measuring effect of gravity by mercury.

Climbing in higher altitudes gravity effect should decrease. It should not have same force, as on Earth's surface. More we move away from Earth's surface, gravity is weaker. At a certain edge of gravity power field, its effect stops.

If we would be able to measure variety of gravity effect from Earth's surface to an edge of its power field, than we could ascertain variety of a mercury pillar graduation. Let's say that force of gravity on Earth's surface is approximately one gravity unit. Moving into atmosphere to an edge of gravity field it will decrease, and we can suppose, that force will be 0.1 of gravity unit. At certain distance from Earth a force will be 0.7, 0.6 etc. In direction to interior of Earth it will increase. It will show as follows: 1, 2, 3, 5, 10 etc. of gravity units.

More we approach to Earth's center, gravity force should be higher. It would reach a few gravity units. From the center of Earth to an edge of gravity power field it would decrease. Outside of an edge of power field into celestial space, gravity would be equal to zero.

Pressure of the air is proportional with force of gravity. Gravity creates pressure of the air and it should be constant on Earth's surface. However pressure of the air becomes influent by varieties caused by weather circumstances, as whirl of atmosphere. 1,000 mill bars should be used, as one gravity unit.

Stability of a ship and airplane, and other similar cases are actually parameters of gravity. Center of gravity of a body is the point where gravity affects. Disorders of these parameters of gravity causes turn over of an object.

MAGNETISM

Soft iron is a matter that receives magnetic induction. Induction directs in sense of magnetic field, and it acts as magnet by itself. Magnetic bar is free from influence of gravity, because it lies on a tiny support in the center. It has freedom of turning, and directing to the poles of Earth magnet. Earth magnet induces magnetism in the bar, and determinates its poles. The bar hovers in the space being free of gravity influence. It takes direction of Earth magnetism N – S.

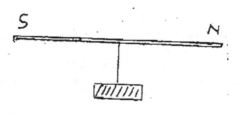

Magnetic bar lays on a tiny support. It is free from influence of gravity.

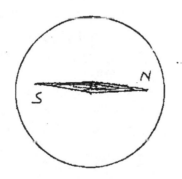

Compass card.
N – S bar directs to the sense of magnetic poles.

Earth gravity shows intention to attract both sides of the bar, but the body lies on a tiny support. It is free from influence of gravity. The bar hovers in the space, and it takes a direction of Earth magnetism N – S.

Earth magnetic field is directed N – S, actually in direction of the axis of Earth rotation. Rotating whirl force forms electrical field, which is in the same time field of gravity, and it shows electromagnetic characteristics.

The difference of gravity and Earth magnetic field manifests in it, that gravity is evident like a force. It affects all matters equally, and attracts them to the center of Earth. Opposite electro magnetic field inducts magnetism in certain instruments, like compass, and gyro compass, or in matters like soft iron.

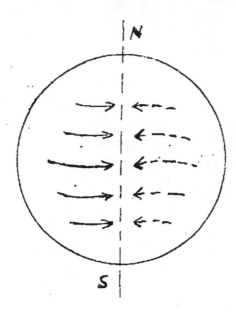

Formed Earth's electrical field.

Gyro compass is gyroscope that rotates at high speed, being free of gravity influence. It is freely hovering in space, and it takes direction of Earth's magnetic field.

Magnetic bar is only partially free of gravity influence, regarding to its foothold on one tiny point. A bar directs into direction of the strongest Earth's induction, i.e. into resultant magnetic field N-S, and equates with the direction of Earth axis. Magnetic bar shows resultant effect of gravity, i.e. N-S poles, as in such direction magnetic induction is the strongest.

If we bring magnetic bar in vicinity to another magnet, it will change direction and assume new influence. A bar will direct in the sense of new stronger field, and it will deviate from Earth's one.

Formed induction of Earth's magnetism already exists in soft iron. Power of magnet is so strong, that it attracts a bar to itself. A bar partially looses influence of gravity and it deviates from N-S axis.

Here it has appeared one, new stronger magnet, whose induction has overpowered strength of gravity, and has attracted magnetic bar. The bar sets into a resultant direction in relation to soft iron.

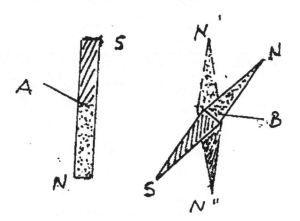

A – Soft iron. B – Resultant direction of Magnetic bar.

Any magnetism forms poles that show direction of magnetic field. For example axis of electro motor, producing electrical power forms magnetic field. Direction of a newly formed field is the axis itself.

Here can be seen similarity with Earth's magnetism. Earth's axis is direction of the effect of magnetic field, whose poles are N-S. A direction of an effect of magnetic field at electro motors is a line of its axis.

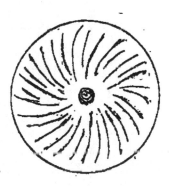

Circular magnetic field is a result of rotation of electro motor axis.
Vectors direct to a center of rotation.

Electricity that is passing through an electric thread, for example a wire makes electric field around it. A field is circular, and a direction is set by a course of same wire.

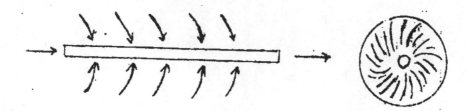

Magnetic field of an electrical lead.

Electrical Magnetic field is identical as Earth's one. It is created by turning force of rotation of axis of electro motor, or flow of electricity throughout a wire.

Earth's magnetism can be compared to electrical one. Concentration of magnetism can be explained by imagined spindle-shaped body, that is widest at Equator, but it diminishes in a direction to Poles.

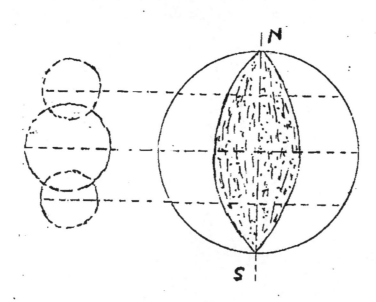

Imagined body of concentration of Earth's magnetism.
Intersection of a circle is broadest in a plane of equator.

On the equator magnetic bar is parallel with Earth's surface. Depending on geographic latitude northerly, or southerly it will close angle α with tangent on Earth's surface.

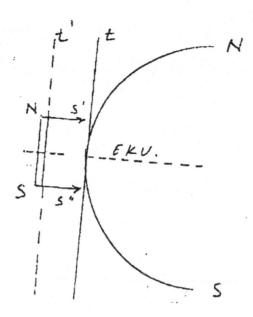

Magnetic bar on equator. S' and S" are vectors of Gravity,

The bar stands parallel with tangent - t. An angle α is equal to zero. Vectors of magnetic force set regularly. Bar stands in direction N – S.

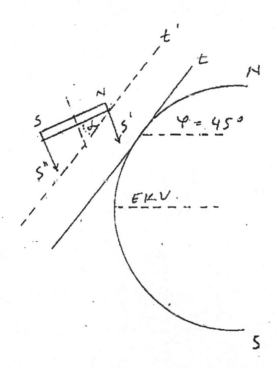

Magnetic bar at 45° north geographic latitude.

Vectors of magnetic force S' and S'' set irregularly. Magnetic bar closes an angle α with tangent – t at Earth's surface. Northern pole is attracted stronger to the center of concentration of magnetic field.

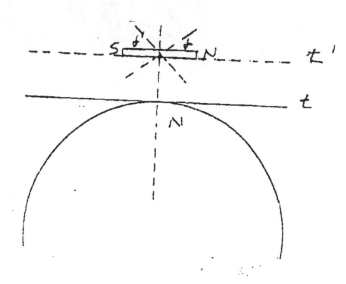

Magnetic bar at Pole.

On the Pole magnetic bar is unusable. Vectors of gravity act irregularly to poles of the bar. They intend to attract the poles to the strongest concentration of the force, i.e. to the center of Earth.

Angles with tangent "t" α and α' are diverse. Force transfers from one to another pole. The bar cruises, and it turns in a circle. Gyrocompass behaves similarly.

Magnetic bar will always show Polar Star, as mark of North Pole. Magnetic N – S line deviates of azimuth to Polar Star.

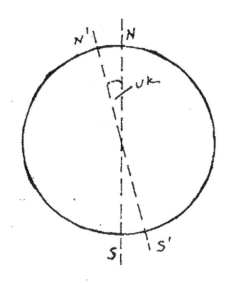

Deviation of compass is high at higher latitudes, as magnetic bar follows magnetic pole, and deviates from the right north.

Earth's axis is variable and direction of magnetic field too. Diversity of error from equator to pole can be considered as geographical factor of changeability of compass total error.

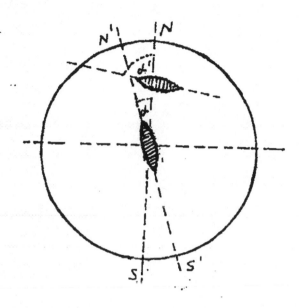

α' is bigger then α. Reason is higher latitude, and deviating angle from right north will be bigger.

LIGHT

Cooling and hardening of a planet takes long standing. Many planets are only partially cooled. Glow, liquid mass is doing constant emission of energy into celestial space. Depending on a firmness of surface layer, an emission of energy of particular intensity will be carried out.

Constant explosions of particles of glow, liquid mass in interior of a planet create an emission of energy. A motion of energy in the space occurs at high speed and in linear direction. Newly emerged beams of light do not meet any resistance. Their speed is defined by energy resulted from explosiveness of a matter.

Energy of the Sun transforms into beams of light in the air mass of atmosphere, as in a medium. Such energy becomes accessible to man's organs. The beams of energy are visible, and we can feel warmth on our skin.

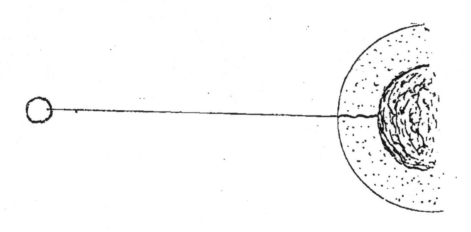

Wave of light from its source, where a beam of light was formed, to Earth's atmosphere.

A wave of light manifests variously from its emerge, until an entry into Earth's atmosphere, where it modifies into light and warmth. Gassy Earth's wrapper acts as the resistance. An essence of phenomenon of the light is a clash of wave with particles of the air in Earth's atmosphere.

Electricity in resistor manifests similar to solar energy. In a glassy tube filled by a gas, electricity will transform into a visual effect. Besides, it will irradiate some warmth.

Glassy tube filled with a gas that will transfer electricity into the light.

Similarity between solar energy and electricity is noticeable. Rotating motor produces electro magnetic force. Energy is whirly, because it is formed on such way in a motor. Opposite solar energy spreads out from the Sun in linear direction.

Electricity has an impulsive character. It transmits by a metal, as medium. Part of electricity vanishes in a surrounding air mass. A sense of the wire as electrical source directs electricity linearly. This way electricity changes its whirly character, and it begins to spread linearly.

In particular resistors electricity assumes a character of light and warmth. In such case it is similar to the solar energy that transforms into light and warmth in Earth's atmosphere.

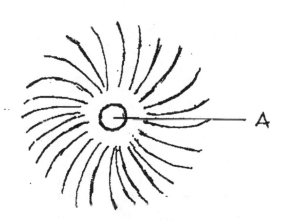

A. Axis of electro motor
Whirly character of electricity.

Gassy Earth wrapper is electrical resistor in which solar energy spreads out, and shows as light and warmth. Emission of energy formed on a far celestial body passes celestial space throughout non medium, actually non airy space.

Emission of solar energy spreads out through celestial space nearly, or totally linearly. Energy that arrives to Earth's atmosphere assumes form of waves. It means that due to resistance, and friction in Earth's atmosphere, solar energy will change a form of transit into waves.

Theoretically an emission of energy in non-medium space should totally extinguish. Meanwhile energy is material in relation to the space. It transits throughout the space by strong launching power. Celestial space is airless, vacuumed and non medial structure. Beams of solar energy are material in relation to the space. It means that sun beams will transit celestial space until their points of range. On their ways through the space they will reach Earth's atmosphere. There they will convert into waves of light and heatness.

Sunbeams in particular mediums gain various appearances. For example light has different color when it shows in water. Light is diverse when it is raining, or when obscured.

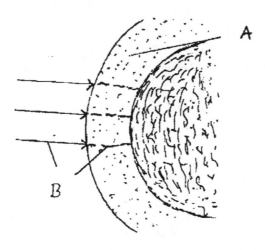

A. Atmosphere B. Wave of light.
Transformation of solar energy from beams into waves in Earth's atmosphere.

We are going to investigate possibility that electrical energy can pass through a vacuum space. This way we can prove a spread of solar energy through non-medium space. The vacuum produced on Earth is different than one in celestial space.

Let's set two metal plates that have a vacuum between them. Let's connect electricity that will be passing throughout a device. On an outlet plate should be registered a voltage, although it is of a lower strength, than one on an inlet plate.

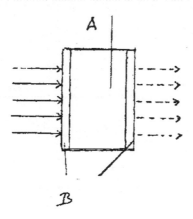

A – Vacuum B – Plates
Pass of electricity through vacuum.

Strength of energy of celestial bodies depends heatness, and firmness of their surface layer. We can sea weaker, or stronger light of bodies in celestial space. Planets with well-developed surface layer also can be visible. Liquid, glow interior of celestial body emits energy in the space.

It is cold in higher layers of the atmosphere. On outer Earth's wrapper is probably less than absolute zero. In those zones energy of the Sun does not transform into the heat. Sun energy has to pass part of the air mass in the atmosphere, as a resistor, that can be transformed into heat.

We could imagine how it would be meeting with solar energy, deeper in the space, and out of Earth's atmosphere. Sun beams could be very cold in such medium. A biological substance could not exist at immense low temperature.

Non-medium celestial space is for us non defined state. Only a biological substance can feel warmth and cold. Accordingly, we can identify it as immense cold state. This means that celestial space is extraordinary cold zone. That is main identification of the space, being extremely cold.

Our contact with the airless space outside of the atmosphere would be immense coldness that any biological being would not be able to endure. Even if we fly with a plane we can easily notice that outside temperature sometimes falls under – 100 C. It means that being in the space we would encounter directly extremely low temperatures.

The Sun is the strongest source of light for us. Strength of energy depends of a source. It means that energy will be stronger, if a source is more powerfully. Such energy will reach longer distances.

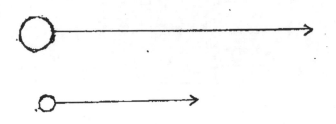

Speed of light vectors of stronger and weaker source.

Speed of light is a product of a power of source. Modern science considers speed of light as a constant. Meanwhile, speed of light is factor of a power of source. The stronger is the source, the light will have more speed, and it will reach a longer range. Range is second component of strength of source.

On Earth we consider speed of light being constant. Such speed is measured on smaller distances. Electrical light is equated with solar energy that is a product of much powerful source. On Earth we cannot observe differences between lights from various sources. We can consider the sun light being emitted from much powerful source, than electrical light. Thaw its range will be much more distant than the one of an electrical source. Moreover its speed should be higher, than a speed of an electrical light.

Here, we are comparing various sources of an emission of light. We can compare a power of sun rays to beams of electrical light. We shall notice that sun energy will reach enormous longer range than electrical energy. Such energy has much powerful source of emission, comparing to electrical one. We could accept that speed of sun light is higher than speed of electrical light, even if we cannot prove it by measuring.

Actually sun light shows only in the air mass, same as electrical light. The light is actually a glow state of particles of the air mass. It means that energy is transiting throughout the air mass, making it glow and visible to us. If we stay in a dark, we cannot see the air mass round us, until a light is switched on. Particles of the air become glow and visible soon after. The stronger energy transits the air mass, the light will be stronger. Particles of the air will be hotter and more visible.

Speed of energy in celestial space is higher then the speed in the air mass. Sun energy transits celestial space with much more speed then Earth atmosphere. We can consider that speed of the sun rays in the airless space could be few time faster, then one in the air mass.

Present measurements of distances from Earth to planets by speed of light cannot be accepted. A distance of celestial body to Earth can be only freely estimated. Ideas can be only based on varieties of powers of the light of certain celestial bodies.

Similar is with a speed of electromagnetic waves, or a speed of sound. These theses can be explained by fired shot. Relatively of a power of arm, a shot will pass longer distance. A speed of bullet will be higher and a bullet will reach longer range. This approves that speed, and range is relatively dependent of source of power.

We can say that the Sun is close to us as it emits strong energy of light. Besides, we can see its diameter that is large. We can see the diameter of the Moon, even if its light is not that strong. If we consider that light of celestial bodies is constant for us, it can give us some ideas of distances to them.

This means that the Sun and the Moon are closer to Earth, than Mars or Venus. The strength of light and large diameter shows us, that the Sun and the Moon are close body. Besides, Mars, Venus and other planets have smaller diameters and less strength of energy.

CONFIGURATION OF LIGHT

We can see pictures, because our eye is such organ that can register light effects. The sunbeams touch elements of our eyes by particles of the air around us. Our intellect determines definition of a picture that we can see. It means that hot particles of the air will hit our eyes to make us recognize varieties of the light. Accordingly, we shall recognize various forms around us.

Dependently on surface layer of a matter, we create idea of color. Varieties of colors are actually differences of surface layers that we can see. It means that various surfaces of matters around us will produce different colors. Actually colors are not realistic but only our idea of surface of a particular matter.

A variety of roughness of man's skin defines colors in our eyes. White, or black skins are actually definitions of such variety. Similar is when our skin darkens during sunbathing. White, or black color of the skin actually do not exist. The colors are only creations of our eyes and brain.

It means that colors of man skins are not realistic. Such skins can be softer, or rougher, or anything in between this two extremes. Being so, they will produce an effect in our eyes that will show white, brown, or black colors. Dependently of surface of man's skin, our eyes and brain will create an idea of color.

We can say that someone has blue or green eyes. The others have black eyes. Someone has blonde hair, besides the other, who has black one. All these colors are actually creations of man's eyes and brain. They are not real, but only ideas that we receive from our brain.

The eye possesses a possibility of distinction of light effects. System of intellect forms pictures. Sensitivity of the eye can be compared with warmth that we can feel on our skin, or with sound, and odor, that we can recognize. The eye can recognize varieties around us that will be defined in our brain.

Energy of light that we receive from celestial bodies is old. Such lights need so many thousands of years to arrive from distant bodies to Earth's surface. Light of particular stars is so old, that we cannot even presume. The view of firmament is formed in the past, being hardly unchanged for millions of centauries.

Some stars are at a same position on firmament for millions of centauries. But what is a star actually? The star could be an explosion of particular body. Such explosion is unchanged for millions of centauries. Liquid, glow magma had not cooled for such long periods.

From time to time astronomers discover some new nova, or supernova on firmament. Main view of firmament remains unchanged for millions of centuries. Stars are at the same position where they used to be in the history. They show nearly same light as in those times.

Rise of the Sun on the east is a vision only. Light exists in celestial space for a long. Earth that is rotating round its axes meets sunbeams continuously. This way it forms an idea of morning rise of the Sun on our horizon.

Stars are far sources of light that compose time integrity of firmament. Picture of firmament has been changeable throughout a history. Light from far bodies is older then from nearer ones. It seems equal to us, because the light exists for centauries in celestial space. We cannot differ, or recognize older, of younger light. Accordingly stars act like certain equality. Alternation of firmament may occur in thousands, or millions of centauries.

Light from celestial bodies arrive to Earth in different time amplitudes. Picture of space is unreal regarding distances of stars to Earth.

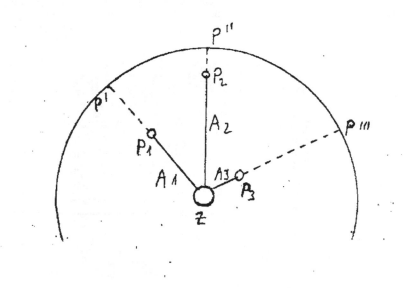

Picture of the space. Z - Earth.

P1, P2 and P3 are real positions of planets. P', P" and P'" are their positions on the firmament. A1, A2 and A3 are amplitudes of distances of planets from Earth. The light temporarily exits in celestial space. It travels for years or centauries from far bodies. If star cools down, and energy of light disappears, it can be noticed only after long period of time, or centauries. That star will totally extinguish for us after many years, or centuries. Some of those stars that we can see on firmament maybe do not emit light anymore.

This fact gives us an idea of time dimensions of celestial space. It considers variety of oldness of lights of particular stars. Accordingly the light of some entire cooled sources still exists in celestial space. This means that we can see stars that do not exist any more. Their entire matter is cooled down, and they do not emit energy any more. But still their light exists on firmament that will disappear after thousands, or millions of centuries.

Strength of light of particular celestial body is characterized by magnitude of light. There are stars of different sizes, as first, second, third size etc. Power of their light depends of distance from Earth and strength of emission of energy. Certain stars emit spectrum of colors, as Antares that is red, and Rigel blue.

Heliocentric parallax of 1" means diameter of a star taken by sextant. This is not sufficient parameter to determine size of a planet. We should know a distance of planet to Earth. Accordingly we cannot determine exact size, or distance of a body to Earth.

Constellations are groups of stars with close bearings of one to another. Their distances from Earth can be various. They seem to us as groups of bodies, and give us an impression of similarity. Their projections on firmament show various figures.

The Sun is the strongest source of light for us. Intensity of energy emission is equal at its entire surface. The spots on the Sun surface indicate that its surface is not entirely red-hot, as the science explains. The spots are actually dark areas that emit less energy of light. It is similar to all other planets. Shiny areas of a planet differ from darker surfaces.

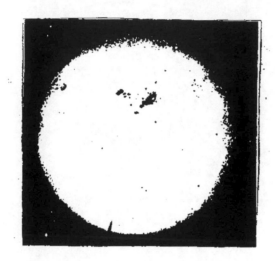

Sun spots. Darker areas on the picture are sunspots.

On this picture sunspots are magnified.

If we take a look at planets, we shall notice that they have dark and shiny areas. This is not configuration of territory, as it is presently explained. Dark and shiny areas are configuration of emission of light of a planet. Emission of energy is done from interior of a planet. Meanwhile, certain parts of body are cooler than others. Emission of energy of such zones is weaker then of other ones. A view of planet with its dark and shiny parts we can call a configuration of light.

Solar prominences are considered to be explosions of a gas on the Sun surface. An emission of energy of explosion of gas is not sufficient to reach Earth's atmosphere. Prominences are actually diversity of emission of solar energy that makes an impression of misty clouds.

Solar protuberances.

Structures of planets are different then we see them. Non-visible planets, for us are entire cooled bodies. It is difficult to notice them in the space. However they emit a certain quantity of energy, that is minimal for us, otherwise we could not recognize them at all.

Mars is partially obscured planet. On the picture bellow configuration of energy emission can be seen. Obscurity of the the body is around 20 – 30 %. At part "A" is probably the edge of a body, as the circle is most significant.

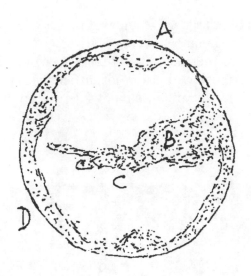

Configuration of the light of Mars.
Part "B" is the most obscured zone of the body. "C" is equatorial obscurity. "D" is assumed edge of the body.

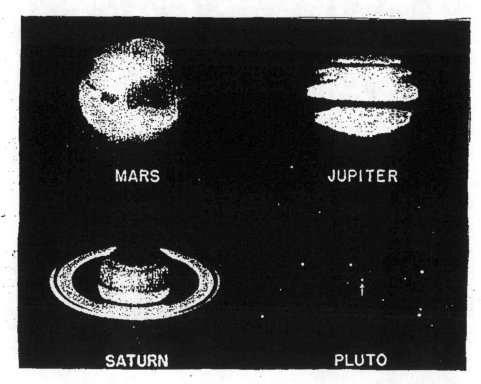

Photos of the planets with possible retouch works on them.

Jupiter shows a flat configuration. Equator and lower area of planet are shown as lighter ones. A, B, C and D are light areas of the body. It could be assumed that 50 % of the planet is obscured. Entire surface accordingly could be larger than visible one for about 50 %.

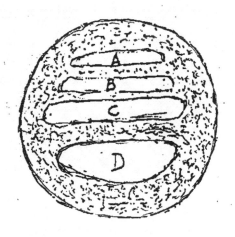

Configuration of the light of Jupiter.

Configuration of light of Saturn shows impression of a disc. It is the most noticeable part of the planet. "C" is light disc that most probably is marking edges of the body. "A" and "B" are also light areas. Disc is most probably a part of the planet, and not a satellite that surrounds Saturn. The body is obscured for about 50 – 60 % of its real superficies.

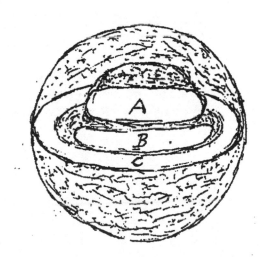

Configuration of the light of Saturn.

Phases of the Moon are explained as non-equal enlightening of the Moon by the Sun. Often there are both the Sun and the Moon upon horizon, but we can see only the Quarter of the Moon. If we accept explanation that the Moon is enlighten by the Sun, than the full moon in the sky should be seen.

We can ask the question, whether the phases of the Moon are not equal enlightening by the Sun, or it is a configuration of the Moon's light. This proves that the

Moon is an active body that emits energy of light into celestial space. An opinion that the Moon is enlightened by the Sun cannot be accepted. The Moon is emitting certain energy that can reach our atmosphere.

Here we can bring some ideas about the Moon which can be interesting. Suppose the Moon is fixed body, and we see its rotation around axis. Than, it will occur exchange of phases, commencing from obscured, over crescent, quarter and full moon.

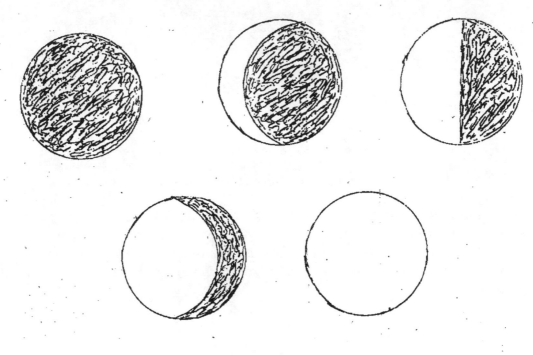

Moon's phases.

Accordingly shiny part of the Moon emits light, and dark side is cooled down. The Moon rotates slowly around its axis, and probably irregularly. At first the shiny part commences to appear. We can see a shy of light over its edge. This emission of energy comes from its active side.

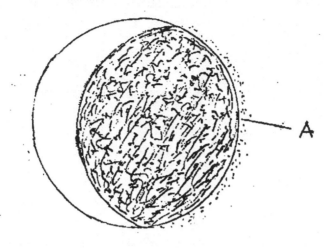

A – Shiny edge
On this sketch we can see shiny edge.

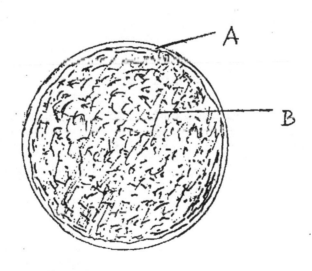

A – Shiny thin edge. B – Dark side of the Moon.
On the sketch it can be seen a shiny round edge of the Moon.

Shiny side of the Moon is larger than dark one. Dark side is irregular. When we see full moon in the sky, than it has ideally circled edge. At certain phases meandering edge between obscured and shiny side of the Moon can be seen.

Obscured side of the Moon is not entire dark. It differs from the sky in the night, and can be seen as a lighter spherical superficies. It means, it emits weak energy of light and we can notice it in a dark sky.

Mercury has similar phases as the Moon. They show its configuration of light.

The Sun and the Moon are equatorial bodies, what means that their positions are somewhere on the superficies of celestial equator, or nearby it. Suppose that Earth is in polar axis N - S. Eclipse of the Sun will be seen from equatorial zone. When Earth changes axes N'– S', we shall see eclipse of the Sun from northern latitudes of north hemisphere. Eclipse is on southern latitudes, when Earth changes axis to N''– S''. The Sun and the moon are situated on the same spherical side of the sky.

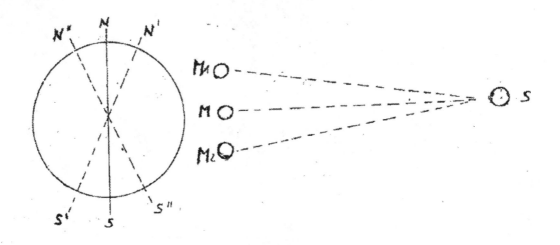

Eclipses of the Sun.

We can see the Sun and the Moon from northern and southern hemisphere, because they are equatorial bodies. Other celestial bodies are sometimes seen only till certain geographic latitude. Those bodies are not equatorial ones, relatively to Earth.

SEASONS OF THE YEAR

Earth rotates around changeable axis that changes yearly for an angle α and α', what amounts 23.5°. Earth sets in N – S line in spring and summer.

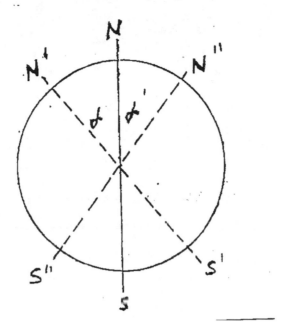

Change of earth's axis.
Angle α is inclination from axis N – S in summer. α' is inclination in winter.

This way become seasons of the year. Science explains this phenomenon by circulation of Earth on ecliptic that approaches the Sun in the summer, and moves away in the autumn. Actually, seasons of the year occurs due to changeability of Earth's axis.
Meanwhile in the summer Earth, by its northern part is the most inclined to the Sun. In the winter this is opposite. Sun declination, that yearly exchanges for about 23.5 ° from N –S axis, actually explain inclinations of Earth to the Sun.

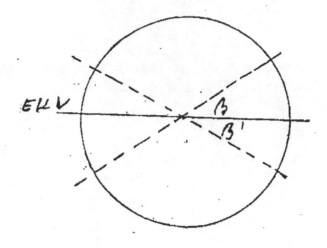

Changeable plain of equator during one-year period.
The values of angles β and β' are of about 23.5°

In the summer latitude of 23.5° is the most convex to the Sun. That is the reason why in moderate zones is hot. Similarly occurs in the winter at southern hemisphere.

Summer on northern hemisphere. Sunbeams fall in under the sharp angle. Weather is warmer due to sharper angles of sun rays. Days are longer because sun enlightening is larger. It means that larger area that includes North Pole is enlightened by the Sun. As Earth is turning around its axis, days will be longer, due to lager area being enlightened.

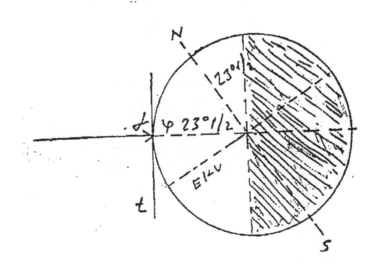

Summer on northern hemisphere.

The angle of falling in sunbeams α on the tangent "t" on northern latitude of 23.5° becomes close to right angle of 90°. Southern pole is hidden to sun rays. Weather is colder, and sun enlightening is less.

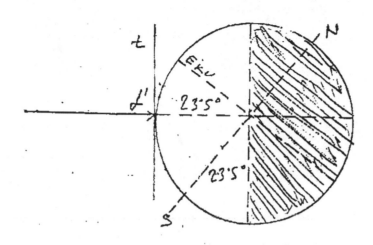

Summer on southern hemisphere.

The angle of falling in sunbeams α' on the tangent "t" on southern geographic latitude of 23.5° becomes close to right angle. Day is longer as sun enlighten is larger. Weather is warmer as sun beams fall under a sharper angle.

Declination of the Sun changes during the year for 23.5°. This proves the changeability of Earth's axis for same angle. Declination of the Moon change similarly, but in shorter time periods, of approximately one month. Certain planets change declinations similarly. Changeability of Venus and Mars is within 23.5°, but more frequent. All this proves that maximum inclination of Earth is 23.5° from its polar axis.

Variety of time periods of moon declination changes, then of Venus and Mars could be explained by improper measurements, and vicinity to Earth. Distances of bodies from Earth influence measurements. Accordingly, similarity of declinations of stars is explained by their distances. Angle of inclination of Earth of 23.5° is too small to influence declination of a body at these distances.

Any variability or inclination of Earth does not influence declination of stars, what could be attributed for the Moon, Sun and planets. Periods of declination of the Moon are shortest, because it is closest to Earth. Similarity can be seen at declination of the planets.

During summer solstice and winter equinox inclination of Earth equator to celestial one is estimated to 23.5°. In period of solstice day is the longest, but in equinox it is the shortest.

Solstice in translation means detained sun and equinox equal nights. In this periods Earth is the most inclined from its right polar axis. In the spring, and autumn

Earth is in its right polar axis. Days and nights are approximately equal. Enlightening of Earth by the Sun is equal.

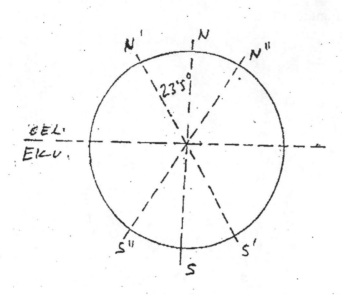

Summer equinox and winter solstice
Polar axis is shifted to N' – S' and N" – S"

During summer period on the north or south geographic latitude, we have occurrence of polar night. In the summer North Pole is enlightened during night, because superficies "P" around pole never sets at obscured side. The pole is inclined to the Sun for an angle of 23, 5 °. North latitudes have short night, and prolonged day due to largest enlightening by the Sun.

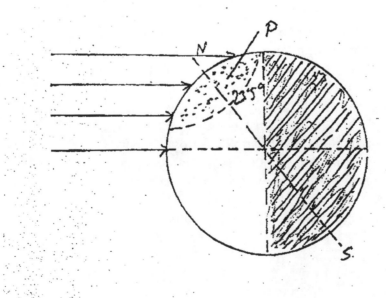

Enlightening of the pole

During a period of one year Earth axis design a circle with spots N and S in the center. Their projections are N' and S'. Circles are noticeable with N' and S' in the center.

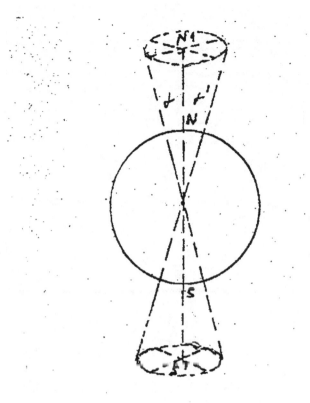

Designed circles of Earth's axis.
Angles α and α´ are 23, 5° each one.

Earth's axis touches all spots of this circle during period of one year. The circles are actually spirals that follow change of the axis from spot N in the center of designed circle.

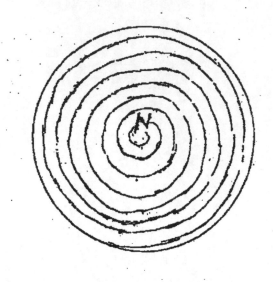

The spiral that Earth's axis designs during period of one year.

The Sun lies at the middle equatorial surface, but nevertheless it is ascended to north, for certain quantity of degrees of latitude. That is the reason, why the southern pole is colder than northern.

This depends on middle rotating axis of Earth that positions vary relating to the Sun. The axis is variable during long periods of time.

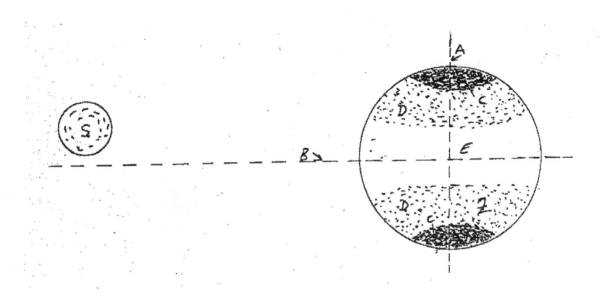

Z = Earth, S = Sun, B= Average value of variable Earth's axis, C= Icy are,
D= Temperate zone, E= Warm zone

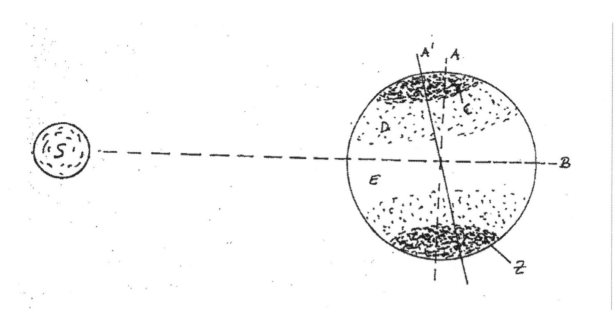

A= Average value of variable Earth's axis
A' = Realistic value of Earth's axis

     This is an average inclination of Earth to the Sun, in regard to that the Sun is raised to north above equator. Northern pole is more convex to the Sun then the southern pole. Therefore it is warmer on the northern hemisphere.

     Provided that Earth changes its rotating axis, it can according one variant come in position, that one side of Earth is warm, and other entirely cold. In this case Earth would have one cold zone, one temperate zone, and one warm zone.

     There are many variants of changeability of Earth axis that can be seen at the sketches bellow.

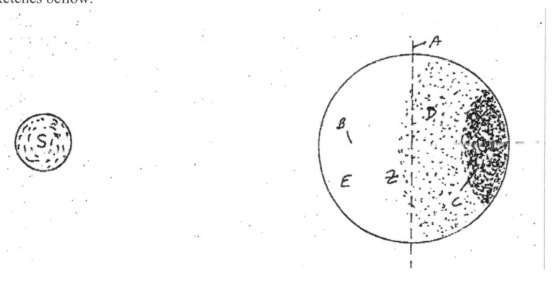

Z= Earth, S= Sun, A= Average value of Earth axis, B= Average value of a line of equatorial surface, C= Cold zone, D= Temperate zone, E= Warm zone

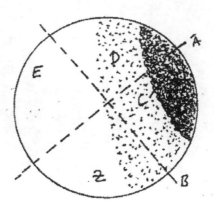

Z= Earth, S= Sun, A= Average value of earth axis, B= Average value of the line of equatorial surface C= Cold zone, D= Temperate zone, E= Warm zone

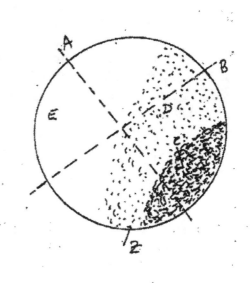

Z= Earth, S= Sun, A= Average value of earth axis, B= Average value of the line of equatorial surface, C= Cold zone, D= Temperate zone, E= Warm zone

SYSTEM OF FIXED BODIES IN CELESTIAL SPACE

On the contrary of today's opinion of Heliocentric System of celestial bodies, here is established The System of Fixed Bodies in the space. Actually celestial bodies are not ideally fixed or still ones. They move in the space, provided that they still own initial launching energy.

We can say that many bodies have not yet lost launching energy, as for example Earth. Earth on its way throughout celestial space meets bodies that manifests in our atmosphere as meteors.

In the space celestial bodies hover or they still move by their initial launching energy. Some are detained, or they rotate, around their own axis. Bodies are of various dimensions. Some are entirely in vicinity of Earth, but others are distant. We do not see them, because they are cooled down. They do not emit any light. Many of them have lost their atmospheres, because they do not rotate any more, and they do not own a gravity field. Provided that a body has fulfilled a range, conditioned by push of launching energy, than a body has stopped, and it hovers in celestial space. Other bodies are moving further on, still powered by their launching energy. Their speed can be considered as a range speed. It is a speed remained to bring the body near to its final spot of range.

Range speed means a speed of body created by push energy that launched a body into the space. A body transits by such speed through celestial space to its final point of range. A speed will be diminishing during transition of the body. On the beginning of push a speed will be the highest. Later it will diminish as the body reaches its final position.

Earth is following its path in celestial space. It will stop when it comes to its final spot of range. Final speed of transit varies from the begging one. Such speed is insignificant relatively to a launching speed that has diminished during a time of transit.

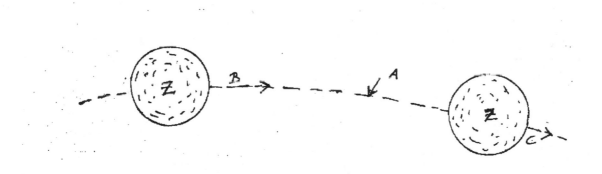

Z= Earth, A= Earth's path, B= Vector of Earth's beginning speed
C= Ending vector of Earth's speed

On the sketch vector "B" is longer than vector "C". Range speed presented by vector "B" shows, that the body has had higher speed on the beginning of transit. Vector "C" shows range speed in the end of transit that is much less.

Particles of gas may remain in the space, as a result of lose of atmosphere of particular celestial body. A gas dilutes in space to smaller and smaller particles, as there is no gravity to hold it assembled. If certain body releases gas from its atmosphere, it will disappear in the space, dealt into tiny particles. If the groups of diluted gas exist in the space, they cannot be visible for us. Therefore existence of gas stars cannot be accepted.

In celestial space there are bodies of various dimensions from tiny meteors to planets of large masses. The number of bodies in space is endless, actually we cannot count them.

Emission of energy of light depends on a size, and quantity of glow liquid mass of a particular body. Size of a body can be mainly presumed only according to its brilliancy.

The Sun is closer to Earth than it is presumed. Therefore, we receive more energy from the Sun then from any other body in celestial space that may have equal or higher emission of light.

This can be understood by visible diameter of the Sun that is large relatively to other planets. More the Moon has enough big diameters, but its emission of energy is much weaker. Diameters of other bodies look smaller to us, what is one of proofs that they are more distant.

The planets of Solar System are entirely, or partially solid. All the planets visible to us emit light. We cannot accept the idea that they are enlightened by the Sun. Their distances from Earth are large, so no reflected light can pass such distances and reach us on Earth.

Actually the light in celestial space has not identification of light. We can call it emission of energy of a certain body. Emission of sun energy that reaches the Moon or another planet cannot be reflected or noticeable from Earth.

Energy in the space has different characteristic then in Earth's atmosphere. Celestial space is cold to mega zero temperature. Sun energy is not visible in it, as space is deep dark. If the sun energy touches another planet, or the Moon, it does not mean that it will be visible from Earth. All depends if planet has atmosphere, or not. Even thaw sun rays can be seen only for inhabitants of such planet, but not for us.

Sun rays can reflect on a glass, or water surface on Earth. But they already became rays in Earth's atmosphere, actually the power of sun energy transformed into beams that are visible for us. Their composition is particles of the air that are hot, or glow. In fact, we can see only glow particles of the air, that we call sun light.

In the other words, if somehow we make hot, or glow particles of the air, we can see the light. Sun, or electrical energy, that is passing throughout particles of the air will make them hot and visible for us. Particles of the air mass are actually resistance that resists to the power of sun beams, or any other similar energy.

Planets of Solar System are totally, or partially solid. All planets that are visible to us emit light. We cannot accept explanation that they are enlightened by the Sun. Their distances from Earth are large, so that no reflected light can pass such dimensions.

Planets of Solar System are situated in certain voluminous segment of celestial space. The bodies have lost their speed of emerge. They are fixed in celestial space. Some planets rotate around their own axis. Some bodies moves on original path at very low velocities. Present motions are totally weaken comparing with their speed of emerge.

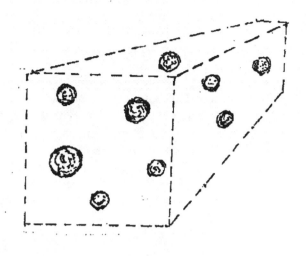

A segment of the space where the planets of Solar System are situated.

The picture presents a segment of celestial space, where the planets known to us are situated. Besides these planets there are many black holes that are hardly visible planets. There are also many other solid bodies of smaller dimensions, that are harden, and they do not emit any light.

We can suppose that Solar System has become by disintegration of a base body. All planets of the Solar System have used to belong to a mass of that body. A base mass that was liquid, and glow matter had cooled in the space, creating newly emerged bodies. Masses have passed process of cooling and rotation. They became spherical bodies that are hovering in celestial space.

Sketch A. Disintegration of a base body. Liquid, glow mass stretches into celestial space. Many planets and other bodies will be created from those mass.

We can compare planets of Solar System with any other group of planets in celestial space. Many of such groups exist in space that we cannot reach by our knowledge. They are immense far and invisible to us. We can observe only planets in our vicinity. Those are the bodies of Solar System. Even thaw, we cannot notice many bodies that exist in our vicinity. They hardly emit any light, as they are partially, or totally cooled bodies. They are dark planets, or dark bodies of different dimensions.

Expression of a dark planet means that such planet is not visible to us, even if it exists in our vicinity. A planet is totally cooled, without any liquid, glow mass in its interior. It does not emit any energy that could be converted into the light in Earth's atmosphere. Even if such planet has liquid, glow mass in interior, emission of its energy is not sufficient strong to show light in our atmosphere. We cannot recognize such body in celestial space. Black holes could be called dark planets, or dark bodies. We can hardly recognize them in celestial space. They emit such low energy that we can still observe them in dark nights. They do not differ much from a darkness of the sky, but still we can point them out like dark bodies.

On the sketch "B" we can see conversion of disintegration of a base body after long periods. New planets emerged from a liquid, glow mass, that stretched out from a base body at sketch "A". Most of planets are dark, and invisible to us. Many smaller bodies are also dark and invisible. Even a base body is dark and invisible.

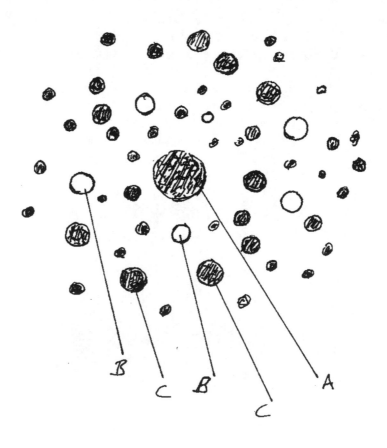

Sketch B
A. Base body B. Visible planets C. Dark planets.

On the sketch "B" we can see many planets and smaller bodies that emerged from a same liquid, glow mass, after disintegration of a base body. We can notice several visible planets marked with the letter "B". Other bodies are dark and invisible marked by "C". A base body is invisible, and marked by the letter "A".

Those visible planets we can assemble like a particular group of planets. We can see only several of them, and we do not know that other ones exist. Such group of planets we can name by particular name, and call it as system "A".

This is a good comparison to understand our Solar System. In our system we can see only several planets. All the others are dark and invisible bodies to us. They emerged from a glow, liquid mass of the same base body. Many of small dark bodies are everywhere around us. We cannot notice them in a darkness of a night. From time to time we can see them being meteors, that arise in our atmosphere.

We can see only the planets of Solar System in the sky. All the other bodies in celestial space that are visible to us are the stars. There are many systems that are similar to Solar System, but we cannot see them. They are far away from Earth, and their emission of energy is too weak to reach our atmosphere.

Earth is fixed and still body in celestial space. It rotates around its own axis. Earth still moves on its path of emerge throughout the space. On its way Earth meets solid bodies that become meteors, whose burnings we can see in the night atmosphere.

We can observe that direction of Earth axis is permanently aimed into North Star. Any movement of Earth will not change the direction to North Star, as it is so immense distant from Earth. If Earth does any precession in its movement, it will not change the direction to North Star. Stars are very far from Earth so angles with them will remain the same, even if Earth does movement on its path.

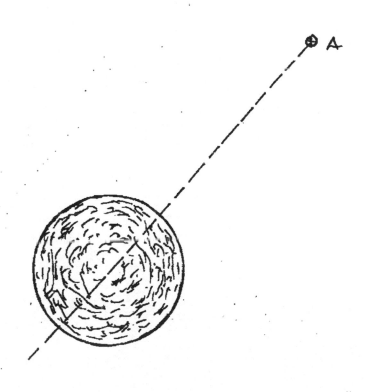

A= North Star

69

Changeability of Earth's axis and Earth's precession does not manifest much in angle α, between Earth's axis N – S and North Star. Due to distance from North Star to Earth, angle α for us on Earth is immeasurable, actually equal to zero.

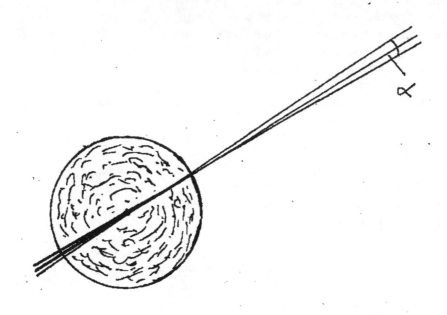

α – The angle of precession between Earth's axis and North Star.

Accordingly, we can understand that North Star is so much distant from Earth. Any movement of Earth cannot influence direction to North Star. Same is with other stars that are also so much distant from Earth. All angles that Earth is closing with such stars will remain the same, even if Earth is moving in certain direction. This occurs due to enormous distances of stars from Earth. The distance that Earth is passing is so small, that angles between the two positions of Earth on its path cannot be observed from a certain star.

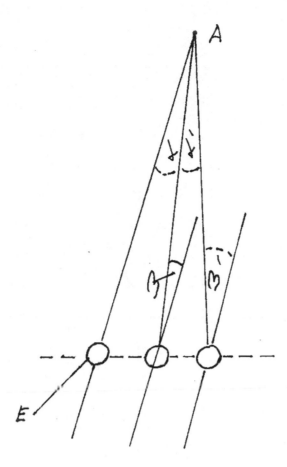

E. Earth A. North Star

On the sketch, Earth is following its path. Azimuth to North Star is constant, although it should be changed, for values α and α'. Earth axis is closing angles β and β' with azimuth to North Star. Angles α and α' are not existing, because Earth is showing always the same azimuth to North Star. Same angles β and β' do not exist, as Earth axis shows constantly right north,

If something is moving on Earth, than changing of azimuths to fixed point can be observed. If fixed point is North Star, changing of azimuths will not occur. Azimuth to North Star will constantly show right north.

A reason is that North Star is enormous far. Changing of angles due to the movement of Earth will not be observed in comparison with such distance. Entire area of Solar System is so small in comparison to distance to North Star, that it seems like one small invisible point. If something is moving inside such small point, no azimuth to North Star can be observed.

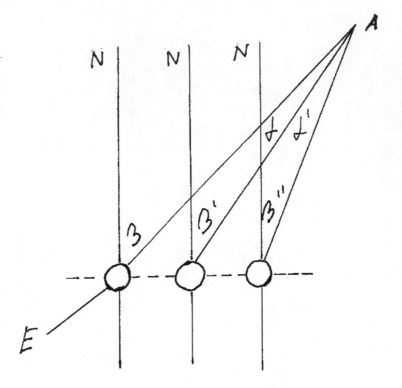

E. Earth A. Star

On the sketch above Earth transits on its path throughout celestial space. Angle of azimuth β will remain constant. Angles β, β' and β" will be constant. No change of azimuth will be observed.

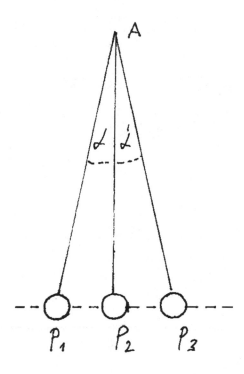

P1, P2, P3 Positions of Earth. A. North Star

On the sketch above Earth transits on its path through positions P1, P2 and P3. Angles α and α' that show changeability of azimuth taken from North Star, do not exist. Looking from North Star, entire Solar System is only one point. Any change in a small area will not show any angle of azimuth.

Present explanation that planets circle on elliptic paths around the Sun here cannot be accepted. The Sun is considered as central body of Solar System. Kepler's laws determine this theory that calculate elliptic Earth's path. The results are correct from aspect of mathematical calculations of ellipse. Meanwhile, here I want to say that there is not ellipse of Earth's path.

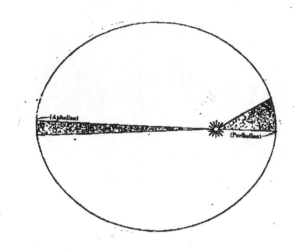

The picture shows second Kepller's law of equal surfaces and changeability of
Earth's speed, at individual positions of the ecliptic path as ellipsis.

A certain power is needed, so that one body can circle around another one. Mechanics in celestial space differs from Earth's mechanics. We cannot implement physics from Earth into the space. All forces on Earth are influenced by gravity.

Energy is needed, so that planets could circle around the Sun. The Sun is the most probably totally still body, that is not rotating, and accordingly it has no gravity. Even if it is rotating, and if it has gravity, the power is not strong enough to influence another bodies. Herewith, we can see that the Sun has no such force that can run Solar System.

If the Sun has gravity, by assumption that it is rotating, then gravity would act to the centre of the Sun. However that force would be too weak to influence any other body in celestial space. Such gravity would be able to attract only meteors that come on sun path, if it is still moving by weak speed remained from its base force of push.

These are basis of celestial mechanics. Without energy, or any other form of power, we cannot accept influence between bodies in celestial space. Isaac Newton's low of relations of two bodies in celestial space does not mention any force. For reciprocal act of two bodies in the space a force is needed. Therefore, these explanations are unrealistic.

A force is needed for reciprocal relation between celestial bodies. Certain planets have only gravity. The field of effect of gravity is relatively small, let's say around 1/3 diameter of a body, or less.

In celestial space does not exist any power known to us that would govern bodies? Newton's lows are mathematical, but they have not any physical postulate or appearances of action of forces in the space.

Only acceptable energy for us is launching force of planets. Such force creates a pushing power of a body, and it forms its speed. Gravity acts to a centre of a body that possess it.

Einstein's theory of relativity cannot be spread to celestial space. We cannot say that one body influence other on the basis of an imaginative influence. Einstein's theory of relativity has resulted on the basis of Chinese opinion of closed circle. Any phenomenon has to be included in such circle. Accordingly any commence has to have an end.

Einstein probably accepts this opinion to explain theory of relativity that relates to everything in the life. Accordingly, everything is relative and it depends each of other, as in science, or in common life.

In those times existence of forces and their influence has been insufficiently explained. Accordingly, the theory of relativity was accepted by astronomers. It has substituted any other idea being sufficient for explanation of celestial space. Those postulates have guided astronomers to form an opinion of celestial sphere without application, and implement of celestial forces.

Herewith will be implemented a theory of forces in celestial space. Such theory wants to say, that any influence between celestial bodies has to be explained by forces. It means if one body in celestial space attracts another one, forces between them should be defined. This is actually the implementation of physics in astronomy. Nowadays astronomy does not show much physics in its texture. It is mostly based on descriptions, and mathematical calculations.

Newton explains influence of two bodies, and their relations without implement of celestial forces. It is obvious that he is governed by opinion similar to Einstein's one. Obviously, this opinion was existing even earlier then Einstein had published the theory of relativity.

It is positive to deny the theory of relativity, and relation of two bodies in celestial space. The science has to go ahead and discover palpable results. The celestial forces should be defined and implemented in the science of celestial sphere.

Solar System is explained similarly. On the bases of theory of relativity, the planets circle the Sun, either in this theory celestial forces were not implemented. It means that planets of Solar System are circling the Sun, without an influence of any force.

We have reached the notion of Ecliptic, as a flat surface, which the planets move on, on their ways around the Sun. However, Solar System is only volumetric segment of celestial sphere, where the bodies are relatively in a still condition. It means that planets are located in volumetric space in certain segment of celestial sphere.

Identified celestial forces can create dependence between celestial bodies, provided that they are existing and they act in the space. We cannot speak about celestial mechanics without mentioning action of celestial forces to reciprocity of celestial bodies.

If any celestial body comes in the field of action of Earth's gravity, it will be influenced by it. Similar happens to meteors. Earth is not ideally still body. During its motion throughout celestial space, it meets bodies of different sizes. The gravity attracts some of them to Earth's surface. The meteors that are passing through Earth's atmosphere incandesce and they become discernible. They simultaneously burn out, and their mass diminishes. That is why we cannot establish original dimension of meteor's previous body, neither of its shape. Most probably some meteors have had larger dimensions before being burned out in the atmosphere.

On the basis of this gravity is identified celestial force. Gravity can attract another celestial body, if it comes in its field of its action.

We could ask a question, what conditions of life are on the Moon? The rotation of the Moon is most probably weak, or it does not rotate at all. Accordingly the Moon has no atmosphere. Such condition of a celestial body hardly can be defined by our knowledge.

It is hard to say what the temperatures on the Moon are. If the body emits energy of light, than at least part of its surface is hot. The zones that do not emit energy are most probably cold areas. Same as the Sun, the Moon has red hot and cold zones. The dark zones on the Moon surface are the zones of a weaker emission of energy.

On the sun surface we can notice sun spots that are the zones of weaker emission of energy. If we assume that whole surface of the Sun is red hot, than sun spots are surfaces of weak emission of energy. The planets of Solar System show same configuration on their surfaces. We can observe shiny and dark zones on them. Shiny zones are the areas of stronger emission of energy.

Nearly whole superficies of the Sun is red hot. Only few sun spots show tiny dark areas on it. The Moon and the planets show more dark areas on their superficies. It means that they are colder than the Soon.

We can suppose that the Moon is close body. Therefore we can conclude that its emission of energy is weaker than emission from the Sun. But planets of Solar System are not so close bodies. What would be emission of energy, if they are closer to us, we can hardly assume. Accordingly any planet in Solar System can be the sun for another body, if it has enough strong emission of energy of light.

The life on the surfaces of all visible planets is most probably impossible. The temperatures are very high, and any kind of life cannot exist. Man or any human device can hardly reach the surfaces of these bodies. Their superficies are red hot having very high temperatures that man cannot endure.

Many planets of Solar System are not visible to us. Those planets, that we can hardly notice in celestial space, we can call black holes. Someone of such black holes may have similar conditions on its superficies as Earth. In such case the life would be possible on that body.

Earth hardly emits any energy that can be visible in celestial space. If we travel in the plain throughout the atmosphere, on the opposite side of the Sun we can hardly see the surface of Earth. It means that Earth is a black hole like many others in Solar System.

If we travel to the higher altitudes, we shall notice that it becomes colder and colder. This means that away from Earth's atmosphere is very cold, most probably much colder than absolute zero. Biological substance cannot exist in such conditions.

Celestial space is immensely cold. Coldness is its basic characteristic. The sunbeams, prior entering Earth's atmosphere were cold. They transform into light and warmth only inside Earth's air wrap.

Definition of sun energy in celestial space, away from Earth's atmosphere could be equated with electricity. Electrical energy being outside of a resistor does not show any light. Its warmth is dependent of a conductivity of resistor. A contact of electrical energy with the human body we feel as a stroke. Simultaneously a human body becomes a lead and resistor.

Some quantities of electrical energy that fritters away from a lead into outside air are not so much danger for the man any more. The air mass is not that good electrical medium as a wire. Electricity in the air mass will hardly be able to cause any injury to a man. Only if man comes to close to a wire, than he will feel electrical shock. It means that even in the air electricity can be dangerous.

A voltage that electricity has in a lead will reduce in the air mass for many times. A lead is proper medium where electricity voltage can rise. In the air mass electricity fritters away, and its voltage falls. In the same time it becomes less danger for man.

If electricity transits vacuum space, than its voltage will be less then in the air mass. Its particles will not meet any resistance in such space. Electricity will transit vacuum space under very low voltage, comparing to same energy in a lead.

Electrical energy being in vacuum can be compared to solar energy in celestial space. Sun beams most probably have low voltage when transiting the space in vicinity of Earth. In Earth's atmosphere they confront to resistor of the air mass, where they show power of the light and warmth.

This rule is valid only for transit of sun energy in area of vicinity to Earth. What is a voltage of sun energy close to the Sun? Most probably sun energy has very high voltage in vicinity of the Sun. Such energy spreads out throughout the coldness of the space. Its voltage diminishes with a distance from the Sun.

A material particle of sun energy is hot. Being material in the same time means being hot. Such hot particle transits celestial space. A particle is still hot when it touches Earth atmosphere. If particle was not hot, it would not be existing any more. It would remain somewhere in the space, like many others, that have been sent from the Sun. Its material state would convert into non material coldness of celestial space.

Vicinity of the Sun is the most probably hot due to a strong emission of energy. The most probably large quantities of gas are exploding on sun surface, sending energy into celestial space. Such energy heats closer area around the sun. Afterwards sun rays transit throughout coldness of celestial space.

The Sun is emitting large quantities of hot energy. It means that gassy particles are sent into celestial space. They transit space like gassy, material elements on their way to Earth, or even further on. Some of them loose their voltage and mass, having no strength to transit the space any more. Other ones proceed to transit until their final point of range. There they will loose their voltage and mass. They will become part of non material, and cold celestial space.

Transit of electricity produced on earth can explain similarities to transit of sun energy. Electricity is transiting through lead wire, having particular high voltage. Such electricity will come to antenna that will send it into the air mass. Electricity will loose its voltage and character. It will convert into electromagnetic waves, and continue to transit throughout air mass. Particles of air will become carriers of electromagnetic waves. They will carry new form of electricity throughout the air mass by motion. In the other words particles will be moving, and touching each – other, caring electromagnetic energy throughout the air mass.

Such electricity, being electromagnetic waves, still has voltage, otherwise it would die. When electromagnetic waves pass border of atmosphere, they will reach into celestial space. If those waves still have voltage, they will transit space. A particle of the air mass is not carrier of force any more. It will convert into material particle of energy, being launched into the space. Such particle will transit the space until its final point of range. There material particle will loose all material characteristics, and become part on non material celestial space.

Accordingly for transit of energy in celestial space it is valid only a rule of launching. It means that a material particle has to be launched into the space, in view to carry electromagnetic waves throughout such zone. No any other rule can be valid in the space, besides of launching. In non material celestial space only mode of launching can be used for transit throughout of it.

If we want to transit celestial space in a space ship, than we have to use mode of launching. That is the only way how we can reach into such zone. Transit of such space vessel throughout celestial space would be similar to transit of sun energy through it. Such vessel would be following straight path until its final point of range.

Rising to the higher elevations of atmosphere conditions of life becomes unfavourable. The temperature becomes lower and lower. Biological organism looses possibility of existence. The materials known up to now can stand the temperature of - 180° to - 200°C. It is not enough to protect biological organism of immense coldness in celestial space.

Our encounter with sun energy in celestial space would be demonstrated as immense coldness. Sun energy is constant, but not impulsive as electricity. During its stretch throughout celestial space, sun energy does not produce impulses, as electricity does. Provided that a biological body from Earth comes into conditions of celestial space, it would freeze.

A light of celestial bodies we can see, due to transformation of sunbeams in Earth's atmosphere into light and warmth. If there was not atmosphere, the light of the Sun, the Moon, planets and stars would not be visible. Similar would be if we observed the firmament from certain position out of Earth's atmosphere. Celestial bodies would not be visible.

A light from certain distant celestial bodies as for example stars, transits for long series of years throughout celestial space. Such light is present in our field of vision, since very long ago. We can hardly imagine periods of millions of years, or centuries, that such light is presented in our atmosphere.

Stars are bodies that are situated at different distances from Earth. We can estimate something about them, according to strength of source of light that they emit, actually as we can see them. Their distances are various in accordance with Earth.

We can talk about time depth of celestial space, accordingly how long time the light needs to reach Earth. Respectively how long are lights of particular celestial bodies present in surroundings of Earth. We come to the point of various ages of light. Accordingly we can say that some lights are younger, and others are older ones.

It means that a light of particular star is on firmament for thousands of years. A light of another star is on firmament for millions of year. Every star that is projected on firmament has different age of light. Any light of a star that we can see is younger, or older than other one.

Projection of stars' lights on firmament is equal to us, even if it is characterised by stars of stronger and weaker intensity. Actually projection shows time intensity of light, whether light on firmament is younger, or older.

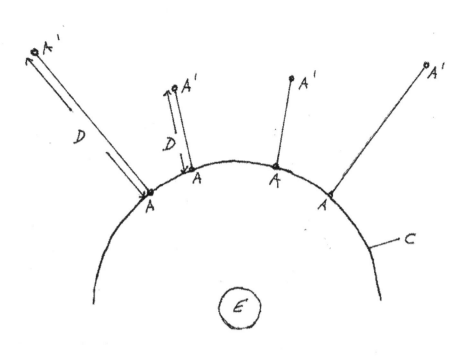

A. Projection of a celestial body on firmament. A'. Real position of a celestial body. C. Firmament. D. Celestial depth of a body. E. Earth.

We can imagine that firmament is close to us, just over Earth's atmosphere. Positions of celestial bodies are deep in celestial space. A' are not real positions of bodies. Those are positions where once bodies used to be. Some of them already disappeared, but their energy still exists in celestial space.

Lights of celestial bodies on celestial sphere can be young, or old. It means how old a source of light or a star is. Does particular star still exists in its original appearance, or not? The light can exist on firmament, even if a star disappears, or actually transforms. That star we can call a dead star, even if its light shows on the sphere. In other words, dead star means that a star as source of energy died. The star disappeared from celestial space, but its light still shows on firmament.

Young light means that a new celestial body appeared on firmament. Old light means that particular star maybe disappeared for millions of years ago, but its light still exists.

An age of celestial light means a period of time, since such light was observed on firmament. Some lights can be old for thousands of centauries, even if their source does not exist any more. Actually here we speak about an age of light only. Celestial bodies that produced such lights maybe do not exist anymore in a previous form. Their light is still visible on firmament.

Here, we discovered a theory of time intensity of light. It means that light of stars or planets shown on firmament is not real one. Those lights come from different deepness of celestial space. Many of those light sources are extinguished for millions of years, but we can still see their lights. Actually their emission of energy still exists in celestial space that reaches Earth's atmosphere. Energy of dead star will transit throughout the space for a long, until one day such light disappears from firmament.

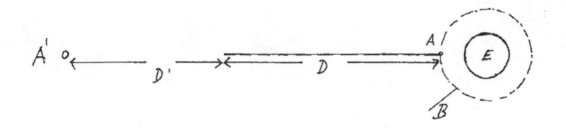

A. Projection of a celestial body on firmament. A'. Real position of a celestial body.
B. Firmament. D. Emitted energy that still exists in the space (Alive Energy).
D'. Energy that disappeared (Dead Energy). E. Earth.

Suppose certain celestial body emits energy in celestial space. The energy will transit space until it reaches its final range. It depends how strong emission of energy is, so far it would reach. Energy will not disappear in the space, until it does not reach its final spot of range. Any particular particle being carrier of energy has to reach its final point of range.

If source of energy disappears, the energy will still transit celestial space. It means that the energy is something that has been pushed into the space. It has to transit throughout the space and reach its final spot of range. At the spot of range such energy will die, or disappear. Material particles, being carriers of energy will equal with surrounding non material celestial space. Particles will remain hovering in space, loosing their material components that they have.

Here we can talk about an alive or a dead energy. If source of energy disappears, or dies, part of its energy will die. Other part of its energy will remain transiting celestial space, on the way to its final spot of range. Such part of energy we can call an alive energy.

Now we come to an expression of a life of energy. It means that source of an energy in celestial space will be born. A source or a body will live for particular period of time. It will emit an energy that will be transiting celestial space. Finally, such source or a body will die.

A life of energy will last much more after its source dies. Afterwards such energy will be transiting space until its final range for long period of time. All energies of light in celestial space have different age of life.

Transformation of an energy launched from a celestial body into a light, and warmth` can occur only in Earth's atmosphere, as resistor. It is only known atmosphere to us in entire celestial space that can produce a light and warmth.

Daily turn of Earth around its axis is determined by the sunlight. It is the time period of one day. Dependently of the season of year, length of a day is various. The Moon every day rises or sets for certain number of minutes differently than the previous day. Here the Moon is considered as a fixed celestial body, and it means that the period of 24 hours, as one solar day is not exact. One solar day is the period between rise, and set of the Sun on the horizon. Regarding that the Moon usually rises earlier, it means that real day is shorter than this one, actually Earth rotates slower.

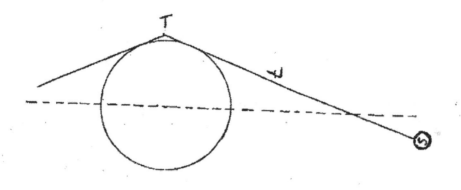

Rise and set of the Sun.

Very distant bodies, as the Sun, and stars increase a horizon of vision. The tangent of visibility "t" from an observer's eye in point "T" touches the horizon, and it extends to endlessness. On the sketch is drawn a middle line, that crosses with tangent "t". The middle line crosses Earth sphere through its central surface. It shows an extension of Earth's central surface into space.

The Sun is outside of a middle line, but we can see it. It is not covered by our horizon of visibility. All distant celestial bodies as the Sun and stars we shall see even being out of a horizon, actually out of a tangent of visibility. It means that day is longer for this difference of visibility that is deviation from the middle line. Such difference of visibility can be expressed in a time period. It is a time needed that celestial body passes distance from point of its first appearance on horizon, until crossing with middle line.

Horizon of vision is valid for certain height of an observer over an average sea level. If we rise higher, a horizon will increase. Than we shall be able to see much more under the central line. In same time a solar day will become much longer. If we rise higher and higher from Earth surface, the day will be longer and longer. Finally if we rise very high, we shall experience only a day light. In such high altitude, it will not be night any more.

Distant bodies increase a horizon of vision, while close bodies are covered by a horizon. The Sun, as distant body, has larger horizon of vision, than the Moon, that is closer to Earth.

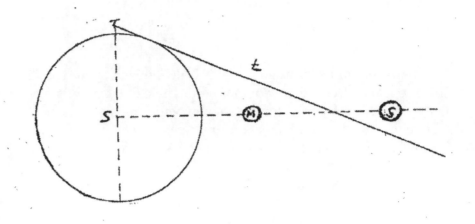

Diversity of a horizon of vision of the Sun and the Moon.

On the sketch we can see the Sun, and the Moon on a same line from the centre of Earth. Observer at point "T" will see the Sun when it touches a tangent of vision, while the Moon will be still covered. During one rotation of Earth the Sun will be more over the horizon, than the Moon.

In a certain moment a tangent of vision "t" becomes a frontier for all endless, far bodies. A rise or set of distant bodies is equal. Planets and the Moon are close bodies. Their rises or sets are changeable, dependently of a horizon of vision. A rise or set of the Sun, or stars for us is unchangeable.

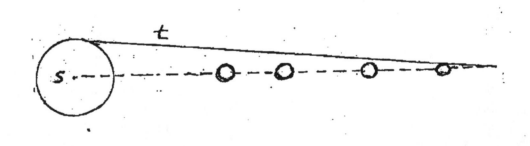

Tangent of vision of distant bodies.

Whether certain celestial body will pass a horizon over a middle area, northerly, or southerly it depends on a position of an observer.

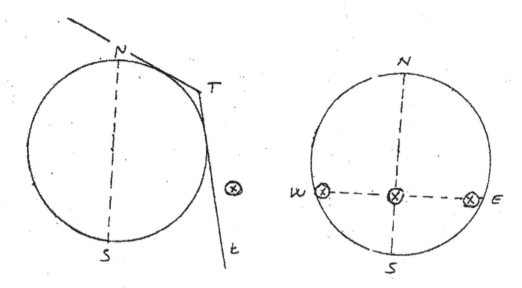

Pass of body over southern horizon.

An observer is on north hemisphere in point "T". The pass will be over southern side of horizon. Those celestial bodies are situated south on the sky comparing to a position of an observer.

The sun is equatorial body. A celestial position of the sun is in a plane of celestial equator, or in its vicinity. If an observer is situated on equator, the pass of the Sun will be over a middle of horizon from point E to W. This situation will vary a little during a year, dependently of an inclination of Earth axis to the Sun.

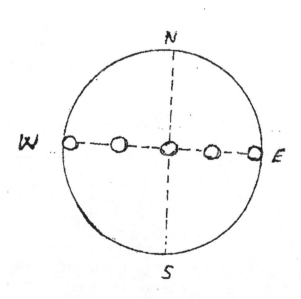

Pass of the Sun for observer at equator.

If observer is situated at northern hemisphere, the pass of the Sun will be southern. Accordingly if observer is situated on southern hemisphere, the pass will be northern. The lines of northern or southern pass are shorter of equatorial ones.

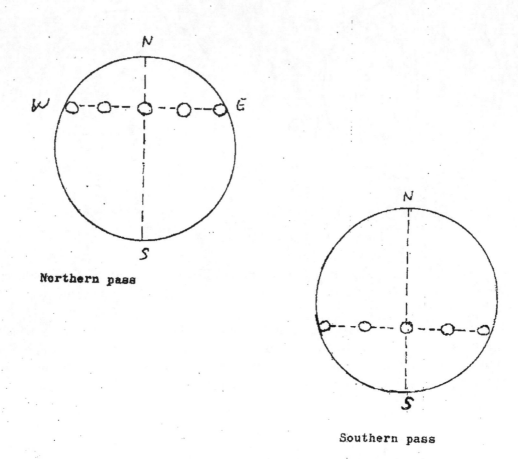

Northern pass

Southern pass

Northern and southern pass of the Sun over a horizon.

This proves that the Sun is an equatorial body. The cycle of a day and night on equator is equalized. On the northern and southern latitudes, differences of a day, and night, for example in summer are big.

Observing passes of bodies on a certain horizon, we can establish their celestial coordinates. This item considers planets, and the Moon. The pass of the Moon over a horizon for a certain observer is always same. The pass will be middle, northern, or southern, dependently on the position of the Moon in celestial space. Mainly, this proves that the Moon is fixed in space, because its pass is equal.

If we rise up to higher altitudes, a horizon of vision will increase. This way rise of the Sun on a horizon can be seen earlier than from Earth surface. This description can be accepted only under condition of large differences of altitudes.

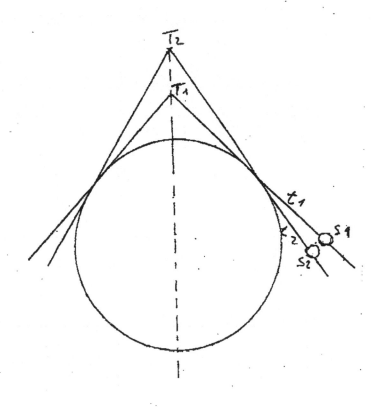

Increase of a horizon by the height.

Point "T 1" is on the altitude of ¼ of Earth's diameter. Rise of the Sun will be in position "S1". Point "T2" is on the altitude of ½ of Earth's diameter. Rise of the Sun will be in position "S2".

According to this we can understand that the time of daily enlightening by the Sun increases with an altitude of observer. If we could be able to climb to higher and higher altitudes, Earth will become more and more spherical, provided that we are still in the atmosphere. The Sun will be constantly visible. It will not be sun rises, or sun sets any more. A day light will be during whole period.

CELESTIAL COORDINATES

Calculations of an hour angle are actually counts of rotation of Earth around its axis, relatively to prime vertical. Declination is angle between celestial equator, and declination parallel of a body.

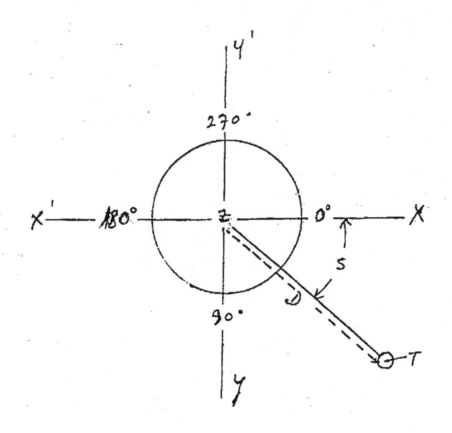

Z = Zenith   D = Distance   S = Hour angle   T= Celestial body
Projection of hour angle. Body is defined by hour angle S and distance D

If we project celestial bodies on the space coordinates we can make a celestial chart. Declination and celestial longitude can serve as coordinates. Axis X – X' and Y – Y' are vertical, and they close angle of 90°. Axis N – S is perpendicular on the superficies that these axes make.

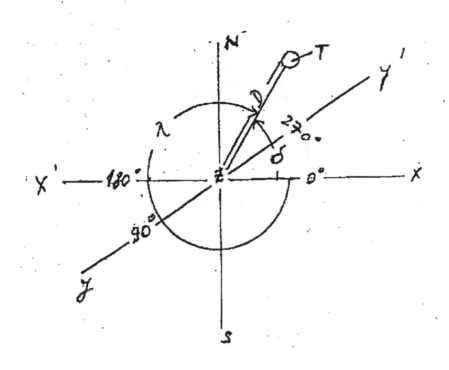

Projection of a body on the space coordinates.

Earth "Z" is in the centre of system. A body "T" is determined by declination (δ), between axis X and N – S, and celestial longitude (λ) between axis X and projection of a body. The distance (D) could be drawn by reduced scale for any body particularly. Angles remain the same, but distances are set to our acceptable relations.

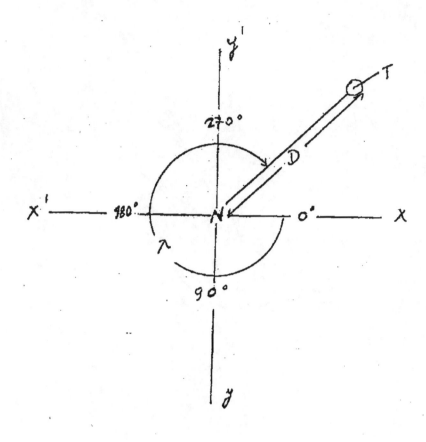

Projection with north in the centre.

If we change present coordinates with new ones, we shall have positions of celestial bodies in space.

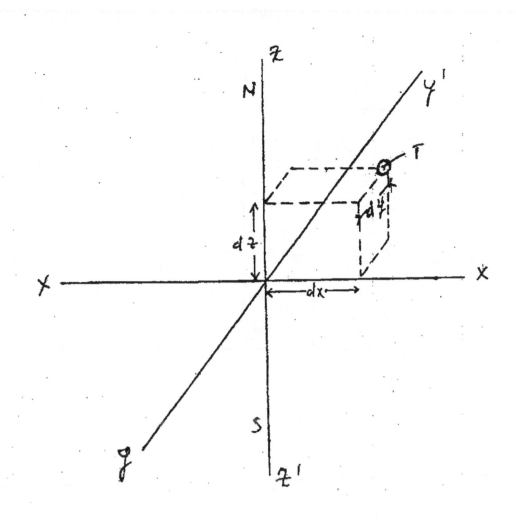

Space projection with three-dimensional axis.

New coordinates are dx for λ, dz for φ, and dy. Earth is in the centre of system. Axis "X" is on the equatorial line, axis "Z" passes through the poles. System is spacious, and independent of spherical dimensions, as now. Projections of the bodies spread into endless, and not to one spherical body. According to this celestial chart for a practical use could be drawn.

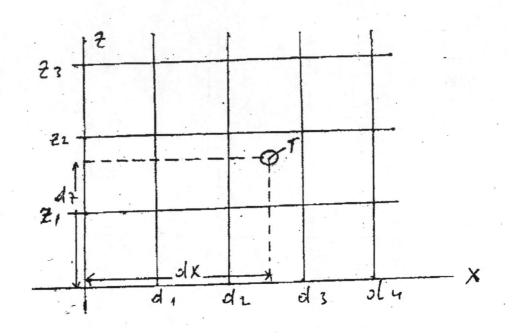

Celestial Chart. It is determinated by coordinates dx and dz.

LOW AND HIGH WATERS

Rotation of Earth creates tides, actually a rise and fall of the water. Earth's rotating force forms a rise of the water that reaches its maximum. Soon, after the gravity predominates as an opposite power to the rotation force, a rise of the water decreases, and it comes back. The science explains that tides are created by gravity of the Moon. The Moon, most probably, has no gravity and have if exist cannot reach Earth's surface, or influence another bodies in celestial space.

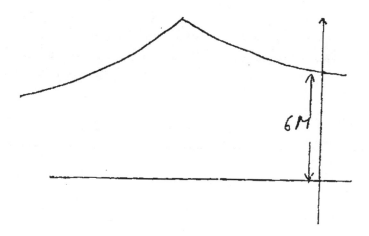

Incoming rise of the water.

A tide wave increases amplitude, and produces a tide, or high water. The water rises over an average level.

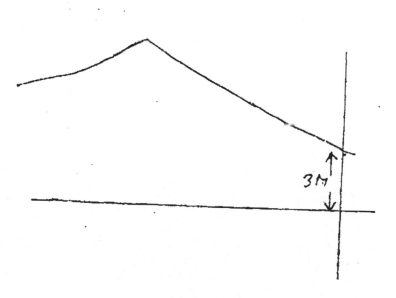

Retreat of a tide wave.

The water returns, and it decreases the amplitude. The effect of gravity results a low water. The water level falls under an average height.

According to this explanation, it becomes phenomena of a tide, and its return wave. A tide is resulted by the rotation of Earth, and a return wave by gravity. The tide wave affects in the direction of Earth rotation. The component of gravity returns the tide wave back.

The configuration of coast causes a size of the tide. The biggest amplitudes are in English Channel, and parts of North Sea. Canal La Manche, with its shape, acts as a funnel. It is situated nearly horizontally to Earth parallels. La Manche is parallel with the rotation of Earth.

Large quantities of water come with a tide wave to narrow channel of Dover that causes an oscillation of tide. Tide wave at Dover oscillates in a certain time period.

Certain winds become similar way, by the rotation of Earth. Air masses are driven by rotating force of Earth that sets their directions. Similar phenomena occur with the sea streams.

EMERGE OF MATTER

Airless, in other words vacuum space is in our opinion empty, or not filled by anything. However, how to describe certain dimension, in which are immeasurable low temperatures, as celestial space is?

We can fill atmosphere as an air mass, actually a space filled by the air. Outside of atmosphere for us a space is empty, as we cannot reach it by our senses. The only matter that we can experience in that space is immeasurable coldness. Actually, a coldness is that, what we can feel, being a biological body.

Relatively still, actually cold matter, if it is heated, becomes reactive or explosive. The most ideal state of a matter is maximally cold. Stillness of matter and coldness are direct proportional. In other words, more the matter is cold, the reactivity of it becomes less.

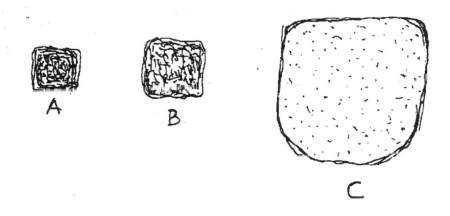

Explosive state of a matter
A. Cold state. B. Heated state. C. Gassy state.

Reactivity of particles of a matter is main fact of increase of its volume. If cold matter undergoes to reactivity, entire mass will increase its volume. It means that a particle will increase its volume, being reactive. It will convert into a gassy state, and increase a volume once more.

Inside a solid matter reactivity of particles is minimal, regarding to a temperature of surrounding. A cold solid mass is relatively in a stabile state (A). If a matter is heated a reaction will increase inside it. In a reaction, it occurs a clash between particles, actually increases of their volumes. In the same time it will increase a volume of entire body. This state we can call reactive state of a matter (B).

A matter burns, and it transforms into a gassy state. Forces between the particles increase volume of a body. A gassy state is voluminously the biggest one (C).

If particles of a still, cold matter are heated, they will increase their volume. Finally particles will convert to their last state that is the gassy one. It means that a volume of particle will increase from a tiny one that is in its still state to enormous large one. This is a base of transformation of the matter. From a very tiny matter, being in very cold condition, if heated it will emerge the mass of a very large size.

A body, being in a hot state, is compact. Its particles are partly solid and partly gassy. If a body loses heat, being surrounded by coldness, it can happen cracking of it. A matter of a body has changed its structure by increase of heat. If a heat decreases, the structure of a body changes again and it cracks.

Here we inspire the question of origin of a matter. The most ideal state of matter is being in cold condition. It means if a matter exists in celestial space on very low temperatures, it could transfer again to a hot and liquid state by an explosion.

A matter diminishes if it is cooled down. Its volume increases if it is heated. Two opposite dimensions come out. One is extremely large, when a body is converted into a gassy state. Second is opposite minimal, relatively solid, cold matter.

A matter that undergoes this process gets dimensions from extremely small to extremely large. We could say that a matter oscillates from dimensions of minus, to dimensions of plus.

If we observe the dimension of minus, or a matter in extremely low temperatures, we can see that body diminishes to less, and less dimensions. We can ask ourselves, where is a border of such diminishment. Let's take a body of Earth's size into what minimal size it can be diminished.

This would happen under a condition of cracking of a matter. A body of composition like Earth is soft. Theoretically, this would be acceptable, however due to softness of a matter, a body would disintegrate and it would divide into less and less tiny particles.

In celestial space, temperatures of endless zero or mega zero exist. The matter that undergoes to this coldness in space diminishes to endless. It means that the certain matter of our Earth's size could transfer to invisible particle. Opposite, from invisible particle it will raise a matter of our Earth's size. These are extreme opinions that can serve for illustration of such process.

This is a theory of transformation of a matter in celestial space. It says that from something small, like an invisible particle, or nearly nothing, can arise matter of large dimension. The condition is a change of temperature, from mega zero, that can be minus 1000 C or less, to extremely high temperatures. We cannot say what are extreme low temperatures in celestial space, even if they are minus one million Celsius.

In Solar System some celestial bodies are heated by the Sun, whether they are large planets, or even small meteors. Actually, they receive energy from the Sun. It depends whether celestial body has an atmosphere or not in view to transfer such energy into a heat. We cannot imagine how a contact of solid body with sun energy is, if it has no atmosphere. Most probably such energy could be felt like coldness.

Solid body is actually a good resistor that can produce certain heat in contact with sun energy. It is hard to imagine if a solid mass of such body can become red – hot. Some bodies are closer to the Sun, then Earth. They are receiving stronger energy from the Sun than Earth. We can expect anything on surface of those bodies.

Sun rays transit celestial space on their way to final points of a range. Earth is inside of a range of sun energy. Sun energy most probably reaches certain range that is more distant then Earth. Energy beams spread out from the Sun until a final point of a range. This volume we can call a field of sun energy emission. Such field can be described like a sphere, as final border of energy range. Some energy remains inside such field on a middle way to a final range, as it has not enough power to reach a full range.

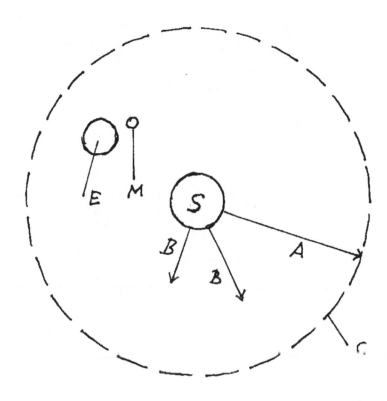

S - The sun, E – Earth, M – The Moon, A – Vector of energy that reaches a brim of a sphere. B – Vector of energy that will not reach a brim of a sphere. C – A brim of a sphere.

On the sketch above is shown a sphere of range of solar energy. Vectors "A" succeeds to reach a brim of the sphere, having more power than others. Vectors "B" do not succeed to reach a brim of a sphere. They remain somewhere on a way. Earth and the Moon are situated inside a sphere of sun energy. They both receive energy from the Sun.

All bodies that are situated in a field of sun energy range receive heat from the Sun. Bodies closer to the Sun will receive more energy from those that are on a brim of the field. If such bodies have an atmosphere, than it will be very hot on their surfaces.

Surroundings of Earth are warmer than some other far parts of celestial space. The sun gives heat to Earth, and other small bodies in vicinity of it. If there is not be the Sun, Earth will become a cold body, covered by the ice. Similar, we can see at north and South Pole, where sun energy does not reach in a sufficient power.

What will happen with a totally solid body under condition of immense coldness? Masses of particles of a body will strive to diminish into less and less ones. We cannot say how small a matter can be in a condition of totally coldness in celestial space. Can a planet of our Earth size convert into a size of a tiny particle?

Opposite, tendency of hot matter is to convert into a gassy state. Particles of gas chop into pieces, and they strive to disperse. In Earth's atmosphere the gravity keep them together.

Outside of Earth's atmosphere the processes are different. If a body explodes in celestial space, newly emerged masses move ahead by thrust energy. They scatter a matter that converts into a gassy state. The particles move away from a central mass owing to the force of explosion.

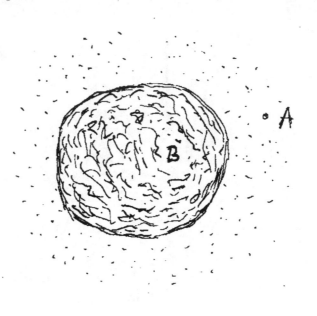

Conversion of matter into a gas.
A. Expanded particle B. Central mass

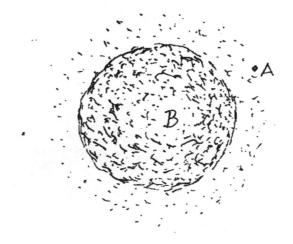

A. Particle at a brim of expanded gas.
B. Central mass converted in particles of a dense gas.

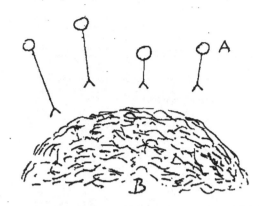

A. Reactive particle moves away from a central mass. B. Central mass.

Distances of particles that reach from a central mass, depend on a power of expansion. If a body explodes in celestial space, the mass transforms in larger or smaller units, which new bodies emerge from. Even if they are small units like meteors, or larger planets. Newly emerged units move in space powered by push force that became from explosion. Some units will pass a longer way, besides others, that will remain in a vicinity of a central body.

Units of newly emerged matter are transferring space having variability of forms that emerged at a moment of explosion. All parts of a matter do not transfer space by equal speed, but they split into new units.

At the Spiral Nebula in constellation Canes Venetici, it can be observed collision of two bodies. Main larger body splits off. In vicinity of main body, there is a smaller spherical body.

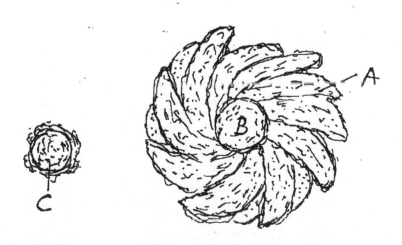

A. Newly emerged forms of a matter B. Central liquid mass C. The body that most probably caused the collision.

Newly emerged matter has a form created by explosion. The matter also possesses motive power that determines its direction and speed of motion, relatively to a range that it will reach. At Spiral Nebula in constellation Canes Venetici, motion of a matter is spiral as it is so determined by explosion itself.

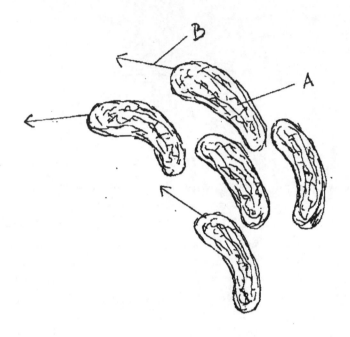

Motion of a unit of newly emerged matter.

Every unit has different direction and speed, although if their directions of motions and speeds are approximate.

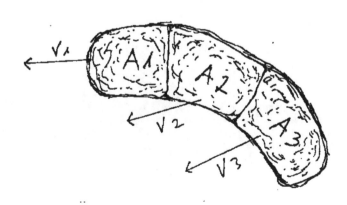

Division of unit of a matter.
A1, A2, A3 – parts of a matter. V1, V2, V3 – vectors of speed and directions.

98

Let's divide the unit into three different parts. Part A1 has the biggest speed and certain direction. Part A2 has less speed and a tendency of change of direction V2. Part A3 has the least speed and a tendency of change of direction V3.

Disconnection of a matter.
A1, A2, A3 – parts of a matter. V1, V2, V3 – vectors of speed and direction.

The matter will disconnect in three parts A1, A2, and A3, that will move further on as separate masses. These parts of a matter will divide and split further on, until motion forces form rotating components that will produce gravity, and make units of a matter spherical.

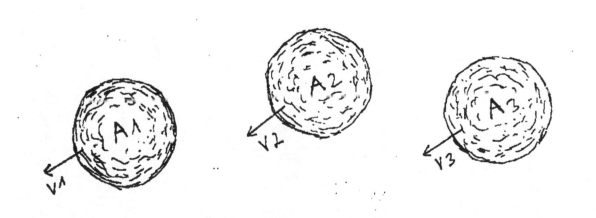

Round off creation of a matter.
A1, A2, A3 – Units of a matter. V1, V2, V3 – Vectors of speed and directions.

A body will gradually cool down, and it will assume a solid form. Particles of evaporating gas will form an atmosphere.

All bodies in celestial space have tendency of rotating around their own axis. A reason is that they do not meet any resistance on their ways that would influence a behavior of a body in the space. A matter in celestial space has assumed a free shape that has become by splitting it. Such shape of a matter forms in long time periods, during its way through the space.

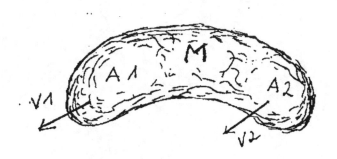

Initial formed unit of a matter that emerged from a base body.
M – Whole mass of a matter. A1, A2 – Particles of same mass.
V1, V2 – Vectors of speed and direction.

Particles A1 and A2 have different speed and direction. Inside certain dimension of a mass, it gradually occurs forming and change of its shape.

Change of a body into elliptic shape.

Vectors of particles A1 and A2, i.e. a direction and speed harmonize. A mass assumes a compact form, and it acts as one body. Vectors of a speed and direction of particles, of those mass on forward and aft side equals.

A body loses a speed of thrust. Rotating force arises. A shape of a body gradually transforms into a spherical one.

Transformation of a body into a spherical shape.

Next phase is cooling and compressing. Surrounding of a body is cold. A matter is hot, and it is still liquid. Particles of a gas detach and they form an atmosphere.

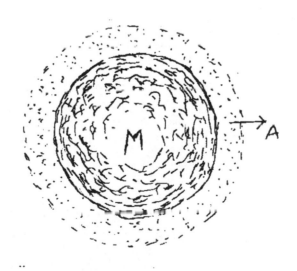

A body in a process of cooling.
M – Mass of body. A – Particle of atmosphere.

When a body looses gravity, it will remain compact, if it is enough cooled down. In an interior of such body a mass expands. If outer cold cover of a body is not solid enough, it will occur an explosion and split up of a body. It means that an outside wrap should be solid, and strong enough to hold inner liquid, glow mass assembled.

If a body that is enough or entire cooled down, looses gravity, its atmosphere will disappear. Particles of gas will expand into the space driven by energy of heat that they content. They will be dividing to the smallest and smallest parts, until they lose entire energy.

Particle of gas.
A – Particle of gas. V – Vector of a speed and direction.

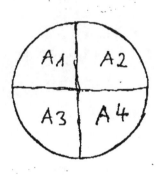

Tendency of disintegration of a particle of gas.
A1, A2, A3, A4 – Formation of new particles of gas.

Losing a driving energy (V) a particle of gas disintegrates. New particles form out of it, with their own vectors of a speed and directions.

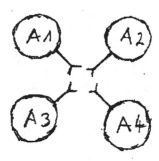

Division of particles of gas.
A1, A2, A3, A4 – Newly formed particles of gas.

Division will take place until a moment when particles loose their energy, which manifests like a heat. It means that they will lose reactivity that they possess by a heat. Cold particle will round up as a particular body.

Cold particle of gas being without driving energy.

A particle will assume coldness more and more. It will diminish, and it will be dividing in tinier parts. Its final tendency is to convert into vacuum surroundings.

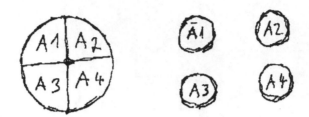

Decay of a particle.
A1, A2, A3, A4 – Newly formed parts of a particle diminish and compress.

It has appeared a force opposite to expansive one that has increased a volume of a particle. Power of cooling reduces volume of a particle with a tendency of its equation with vacuum.

Extremely low and high temperatures are two opposite dimensions. On high temperatures a body explodes, and it decomposes into tiny parts, actually it transfers into a gassy state. Particles are distancing away from a central mass. This way a body increases a volume of a mutual mass.

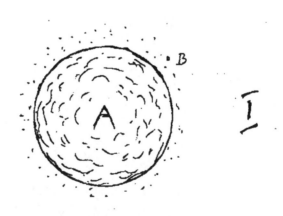

A – Central mass. B – Gassy particle.

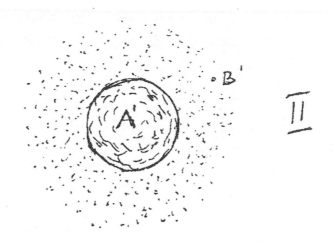

A' – Central mass. B' – Gassy particle.

On the sketch II, mutual volume is bigger of a volume at the sketch I. The matter transfers into a gassy state, and it increases mutual volume.

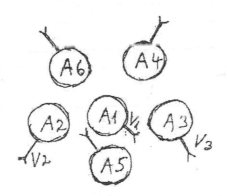

Reaction of a force between particles.
A1, A2, A3 …… Material particles. V1, V2, V3 …… Vectors of forces and directions.

Between particles of a certain matter exists a reactive force. Any particle is driven by its energy of heat that is composed into it. Tendency of a force is to act from a center to brim. In a center of particle reaction is the strongest, because there a matter is the hottest.

This is basic principle of reaction of a matter. Driving energies of particles act so, that they mutually collide, creating a reaction and explosion. It means that any particle that is hot will have driving energy. Such energy will drive the particle against other particles in vicinity. Particles will be colliding each other, creating reaction and finally explosion.

This means that only hot particles can create reaction and explosion. If we heat any matter, the particles of it will become reactive. They will absorb a heat, and transfer it into a reactive force. The particles that are driven with absorbed energy will start colliding each other creating reaction. Final demonstration of a reaction is expected to be an explosion. All depends on the structure of a matter, and how solid it is. Many matters can endure reaction, even being heated to very high temperatures.

The space between particles of a matter we can consider as vacuum. Actually, such space is not totally dematerialized. That is a field of reaction of forces that are driving particles. If matter is hot, energy of particles will create their movements that will fill an empty space between them. This way that space will become a field of an action of particles. Otherwise, if a matter is cold, movement of particles is less. The space between particles will be still and empty, actually a vacuum one.

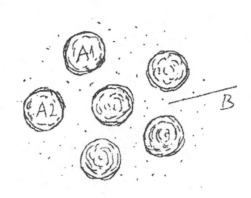

Relation of particles and space inside a matter.
A1, A2 ….. Material particles. B – Vacuum space.

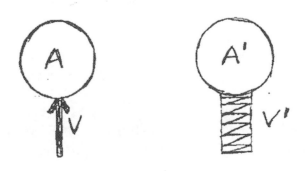

Materiality of force compared with a spring

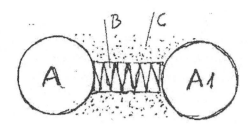

Reaction between two particles of a same matter.
B - Zone of stronger action of force. C - Zone of weaker action of force.

Reaction between two particles can be described by a form of the spring. Whole space between particles is filled with a reactive force. Actually, a vacuum space is filled with a force of reactions of particles. During reaction of a matter vacuum spaces between particles become larger. Volume of entire mass increases. Particles are colliding each other, making a vacuum space larger. In same time they make an increase of volume of the entire mass.

The force is not a material state, but it is only the manifestation of a particle, or particles of whole matter. If matter is heated, its particles will absorbe a heat and create energy. The heat will act to a composition of a particle that will increase its volume. The space between particles becomes small. They will start touching and colliding each other, creating a reaction.

The particle of any matter absorbs energy of a heat that increases its volume. Final state of a particle should become a gassy one. It means that a particle of any matter, even of a very solid one, strive for conversion into a gassy state. A gassy state of a particle is voluminously the biggest one. Volume of a particle from its cold state to gassy one will increase for many times.

This means if we increase a volume of particles by a heat that is composed into same framing, a reaction will occur. All depends on a structure of matter, how it will endure a reaction. Some matter will become hot only, besides the others that will explode.

This is actually bases of an explosion. If we heat a matter inside a particular framing, it will increase its volume. Framing that hold a mass assembled will not endure an increase of volume. They will break, causing explosion of a matter.

REACTIVITY OF MATTER

Molecular theory explains composition of a matter. Actually the theory mentions fine parcels that a matter is consisting from. The molecules are consisting of atoms. Integral parts of atoms are protons and neutrons. Today we can accept this thesis only theoretically.

A matter can be divided into endless petty particles. Division of a matter depends of our technical possibilities. We cannot crumble a matter to its smallest parts. Therefore division of a matter on molecules can be accepted only like a certain imagination.

A particle of a matter is its most petty imagined part. It is abstract and it serves us only to understand composition of a matter. We can imagine division of any matter into its finest parts, actually particles.

Inside the matter of uranium occurs an active process of reaction. A force that becomes by reaction forms an emission of waves of energy. Radiation is spread of waves of radioactive energy by the air as medium. Human organism is not accustomed to this kind of waves, actually to newly formed frequencies.

Effect of radiation to a human organism can be compared to an electrical voltage. A man can endure a low electrical voltage. It will not heart human organism. Very high voltages will keel a man. Same is with radiation. Human organism becomes like an accumulator that will accumulate radioactivity. Radioactivity will decrease, if body is not radiated for a long. Radiation of smaller strengths theoretically could be considered as being not dangerous. Human body would get used on it during a time.

Atomic explosion is similar to others. Uran reacts under high electrical voltage with the catalyst. A temperature of reaction must be very high. Reactive parcels make interior mutual bombarding each - other. Finally occurs explosion of a matter. Newly raised energy releases large quantities of warmth.

Uranium, as the matter, is brought to an explosive state. Atomic explosion can be compared to usual, other explosions. Volume of an explosion is large compared to used energy. Certain quantity of uran can be used for a very long period. Only small consumption of the matter is necessary for production of large quantities of energy.

During explosion of atomic bomb, besides radioactivity, it releases large quantities of energy. Such energy causes an emission of waves of a great destructive power. Newly emerged frequencies are dangerous for human organism that is not used on them. Besides, a strike of air waves is destructive. Such emission of waves, even being not radioactive, is still dangerous for humans.

Next is radiation of a radioactive matter that is used in explosion. After an explosion radiation is spread by air waves to large area around explosion. In this case the air will be a medium that accumulates radiation. Wind can spread radioactive air masses to larger areas.

Providing that two explosive matters are connected, actually their elements, it will occur a reaction that can be from small to large dimensions. A product of reaction is a gassy matter. Newly raised gas, as a product takes large volume, respectively to its primary state. In the case of reaction, pressures increase and explosions emerge. A volume of a mutual matter will enlarge for many times, comparing to previous one.

Here it is visible enormous increase of a volume of mutual masses, that were relatively small, most probably liquid or solid ones. After reaction they transferred into a gassy state, creating enormous volume. Actually, masses are the same, but a volume of their particles increased.

During reaction, it occurs a conflict between particles that are transferring into a gassy state and they occupy larger space. If the process takes place in a form of unchanged dimensions the pressure will arise. One mutual space is filled by particles of enlarged dimensions. A particle of gas is enlarged comparing to previous one of a liquid or solid matter.

How big, or large is a particle is only a point of imagination. We can say that a particle of the gas is larger than one of the solid matter, but it is actually not. Our imagination guides us to understand a gassy state like something larger, than previous solid one. The state of a matter is actually the same, but there are larger distances between particles, that are hovering in a vacuum field.

Actually vacuum is realistic, but particles, being material are filling it only. They strive to become less and less, and finally transfer into vacuum. Vacuum composes all matters on Earth, or in celestial space. It is filling tiny spaces in between particles of any matter.

Vacuum that we mention here is identical to one that celestial space is composed of. It is not a mechanical vacuum produced on Earth that has an ability of suction. Vacuum in celestial space is still one, without any mechanical abilities. Same vacuum is filling all matters on Earth. Particles of any matter are hovering in fields of vacuum. Earth gravity does not attract vacuum, but particles that are situated in it.

Vacuum, being a part of composition of matters on Earth is actually non broken part of vacuum that celestial space is composed of. It spreads throughout matters on Earth, being connected to celestial vacuum. This means that, there is no difference between vacuum on Earth, or in celestial space, and all of it is only one composition. Vacuum, being composition of celestial space pulls through all matters on Earth. Same vacuum pulls throughout all bodies in celestial space.

That is the way we can say that vacuum is realistic. Logically, it is the main structure of celestial space, even if it is not material at all. Therefore, material structures are something that strives to equal with vacuum. If frames of such structures break, particles of it will strive to identify with celestial vacuum.

Reactivity exists in nearly all matters, but it does not express. Actually such process is not accessible to our senses. Ideally compact matter does not exist, but theoretically any one has reaction between its particles. One way of reaction is wear of matter. It shows us that certain process of reactivity is carried out in between the particles of a matter

Reactivity depends on heating of a matter. Hot matter will show more reactivity of particles than cold, and still one. Some matters have incorporated energy in their structure, actually a process between particles that shows reactivity. Such energy is implanted in a matter by it's emerge from liquid, hot magma.

Matters that became from primary hot, liquid mass have not compact composition. It means that they are formations of diversity of conditions in which they had been formed. There is reaction even inside the matters that can be considered as ideally compact. The most compact and most dense matter is a diamond. If we would be able to analyze it, at least theoretically, most probably we would ascertain reactivity inside its matter.

Final conclusion is that all matters are reactive, as they emerged from a mutual mass. They have been cooling down under different conditions, what has created their different abilities. Dependently of their structures, they show different modes of reactivity. Continuous intermolecular confusions characterize structure of any matter. Uranium for example emits perceptible energy.

Any matter is actually a mass of same composition of particles. It has formed in natural conditions from mutual primary hot, liquid magma, as entire composition of a planet. A matter has formed, and it has cooled down in certain conditions of pressure and temperature. Therefore we have variety of matters in the nature. Later the man has succeeded to make different artificial matters. Accordingly whether any matter has become naturally, or on artificial way, it has to be considered as a mass of identical composition of particles.

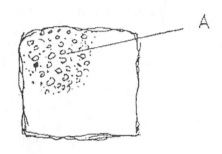

Composition of a matter.
A – Parts of a matter.

Some matters have appearance likewise they are composed of fine parts. This phenomenon could be attributed to a softness of rocks. Likewise we can see variety of structures of matters in the nature. Some are very solid, but the others are soft, even if they emerged from an identical mutual mass. A natural forming made them to be different one from another.

Particles of gas, that become by a reaction, have an impel or reactive energy. They have intention to disperse in different directions from a current position. Oppositely a solid body is a mass of great thickness, relatively to a gas, or a gassy state of same body, that can become by burning of concerned matter. These are two extremities, a solid and gassy state, relatively to a volume that they occupy.

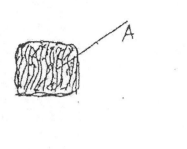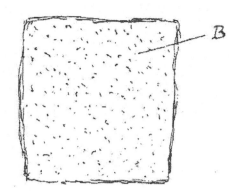

Extremities of a matter, relatively to a solid or gassy state of it.
A – Firm state of a matter. B – Gassy state of a matter.

Particles of a cold body can be considered as still ones, i.e. there is not any visible confusion between them. These idea concerns to majority of matters. If we heat a certain matter, reaction will take place, and a body will expand. Soon it will occur confusion of particles inside a mass of body. A matter will increase its volume inside a same form. In the same time, a volume of particles in such matter will increase. Collisions between them will be stronger and more efficient. Finally, an explosion will take place.

Whether a matter is solid, liquid, or gassy one, it will change its volume by reaction. Even gassy matters will change their volume after being brought in a state of reaction. After reaction, a volume of gas will increase, even if it is situated in a same form.

Explosive tendency of particles is unavoidable, whether it considers one, or more kinds of matter exposed to reaction. During reaction particles will change their state. They will become gassy and explosive ones. Their volume will increase, that will fill a present form, and create an explosion.

This way any explosion will occur, whether it is plain or atomic one. Main point is that the solid matter transfers into a gassy state inside dimensions of an identical form. The gas needs enormously more space than the solid matter. Structure of a form will not resist pressure of the gas any more. Soon it will break, and an explosion will take place.

Here we tray to equal atomic explosion to any other one. We have seen that most explosions took place after certain reaction and a large expansion of gas in a limited form. Atomic explosion occurs in reactor. A matter of uranium is brought under reaction with a catalyst and electricity of high voltage. It means that such arrangement has similarities with any other reaction. Uranium is reacting with a catalyst under high voltage of electricity. Explosions in reactor are taking place.

This means that even uranium is an explosive matter. Particles of uranium will react with a catalyst. Uranium is a matter, that one piece of it can last for long. Even thaw we can observe similarities of reaction, and transfer of particles into a gassy state.

Main characteristic of an explosion is that newly formed gas in a certain form will break a structure of a form. It means that a structure of a matter what was exposed to a reaction had changed the state and it had become a gassy one. A structure of a form cannot hold new gassy volume any more. A form will break under a pressure, and force of the gas. The gas will explode in a contact with the air.

Here we can notice two sections of described process. First one is a reaction, and rise of a gas. Second one is contact with the air, and an explosion. A reaction and explosion can happen even outside of a form. Some matter can react on the open air, and create an explosion in contact with the air.

Herewith we meet an expression of dimension of a particle that can vary. A particle of a certain matter before being in process of reaction has had a certain dimension. State of a matter has been cold and still one. After process of a reaction a particle will transfer into gassy state, and become larger. It means that a particle of a previous solid matter, for example, will change its dimension for many times, and become much larger.

As we know a particle is only imagined, a tiny part of matter. How tiny it can be depends on our opinion. It means that a particle is not realistic, but imagined unit. If we compare a particle of a solid matter that will transfer into a gassy state than normally, it will become much larger one. It means that a volume of a vacuum between particles of two different states will change. When masses were solid ones, distances between particles were much smaller, then at newly formed gassy matter. A volume of a vacuum will increase for so many times, when a matter changes from a solid to gassy state.

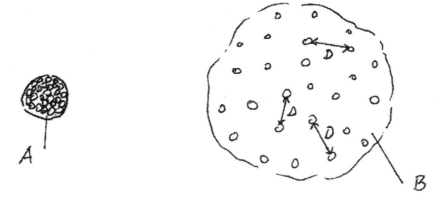

A. Solid matter. Particles are dense. B. Same matter transferred into a gassy state. Particles are distant each from other. D. Distances between particles.

A primary matter has been cooled under different conditions. Its natural form has not been ideally filled. A matter would have been more solid, and compressed, if an underground pressure has been stronger. Diamonds have become this way. Hot, liquid magma has formed under very high pressure at adequate temperatures in the natural form.

This actually has happened on Earth. Diamond is most solid natural matter that we know. But what we can expect in celestial space? Are some bodies fully formed likewise diamonds? Are they actually large diamonds? Have their hot, liquid magma been cooled in a form, under adequate pressures and temperatures?

We know that diamond is only a part of our nature, like stones, or minerals. But liquids and gases are also parts of our nature. We can say that certain planets have become from a same base mass, as Earth has become from. But how that mass has been cooled down? What have been pressures, and temperatures? How, it has been their natural form?

So in celestial space we can expect any kind of a matter. It can be similar to our Earth, or much different one. We can discover bodies formed of a gold, or diamonds. Anything can be expected there far in celestial space.

The view of the Moon in the phase of quarter, where it looks as partly covered by Earth, could be acceptable only, if we could see the Moon from a distant point in celestial space. In this case Earth would be positioned in between the Sun, and the Moon.

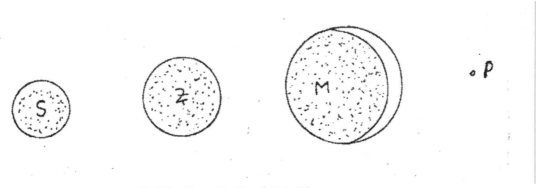

S. The Sun Z. Earth M. The moon
The view of the moon in the phase of quarter.

Looking at the moon from a point P, we could say that it is partially covered by Earth, and that we see only a certain phase of quarter. This solution would be acceptable if the Moon is enlighten by the Sun, and covered by Earth. Such view of the Moon could not be observed from Earth.

We could talk about eclipse of the Moon by Earth that is hiding sun light which is directed to the Moon. Such explanation could be taken in consideration in case that Earth is situated in between the Sun and the Moon. Sometimes we see the Sun, and the Moon's quarter in the sky during the day time.

Besides, the light takes a very long time to bring a certain picture of celestial space to an eye of observers. Sometimes a light has to travel for years to show to observer what is going on in celestial space. We have to take in consideration that the Sun, and the Moon are closer bodies to Earth, than stars. Their light will reach observer in less time, than a light from distant stars that travels to us for centauries.

As we saw earlier, the Sun energy could not enlighten the Moon, neither such energy could be reflected. The Sun energy is different in celestial space, then in Earth's atmosphere. It is a dark and cold emission of power that is transferring throughout celestial space. Even if it touches the Moon, it does not mean that any light will arise on its surface. The light can be formed only in a specific atmosphere, like Earth's one.

A reflection of energy of light can be observed only on Earth. The light on Earth is formed in the air mass that we are surrounded with. When the Sun energy is passing through the air masses, it is touching its particles that are creating a resistance. Particles of the air become hot, and visible to us. They show a light, and warmth that we can feel. Same will happen if we switch an electrical light on.

Phenomenon of a reflection of the light is known on Earth. It means that the light can be reflected over certain surfaces, as mirrors, a glass, a still water, and similar ones. When a power of the light transfers throughout the air mass, as a medium, particles of the air are carriers of a force. They are colliding each, other transferring a power of the light further on throughout the atmosphere. When such composition of a power and hot particles of the air, what we call the light, touches a surface of a mirror, it will be reflected. It will be transferred further on throughout the air mass in a direction of an angle of reflection.

It means that particles of the air, that are carriers of energy of the light will touch a surface of a mirror. Than they will reflect on a glass, and proceed caring on an energy, touching and colliding each other. A hot particle of the air is actually a material matter that can be easily reflected over a glass surface of a mirror.

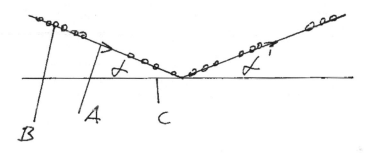

A. Sunray, energy that reflects over a mirror. B. Particles that are carriers of energy of the light. C. Mirror

Here, we understood that real carrier of sun energy on Earth is a particle of the air. When the sun rays touch Earth atmosphere, energy will be carried on by particles of the air. Particles will be colliding, and touching each – other, carrying the Sun energy further on. In the same time they will become hot and visible to us. We should recognize the light in our surrounding that was dark previously.

This means that we can see the air, or air particles only if they are energized by the Sun, or some another energy. In such moment we can say that we see a light. Otherwise we cannot proof that we see the air around us that is actually a dark composition. Our eyes are not such improved that they can recognize air particles that are surrounding us.

We can consider the Moon being a source of energy of light. Is it only a configuration of the light that we can see on moon's surface? Are all those various shapes that are shown on its sphere only a difference of emission of the energy?

A solution that the Moon is a body of irregular shape could be interesting. It means that maybe the Moon is not totally, but only partly a spherical body. This idea can hardly be taken in consideration, as all bodies in celestial space are spherical. Most probably it is only a configuration of the light that we consider like missing part of the Moon.

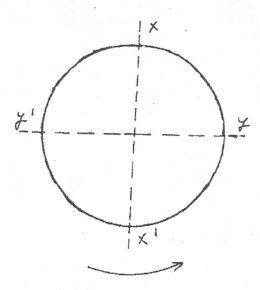

Phase of the totally spherical Moon. The Moon emits full light.

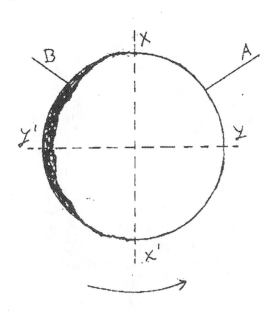

In this phase the irregular side of the Moon commences to uncover.
A. The circled side of the Moon. B. Contorted edge.

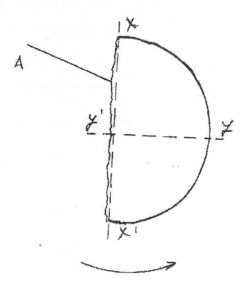

The moon is nearly cut in this phase.
A. Irregular edge of the Moon.

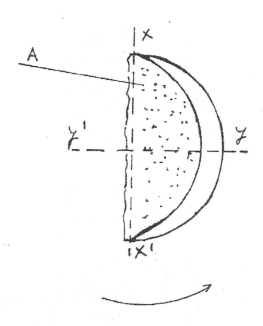

The phase of obscured part of the Moon.
A. Obscured part of the Moon.

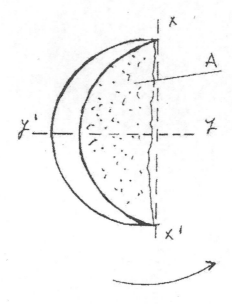

The phase of another uncovering of the enlightened part of the Moon.
A. Obscured part of the moon.

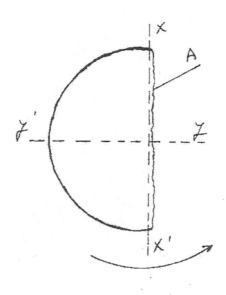

The phase of the Moon being half enlightened.
A. The edge is cut straight.

118

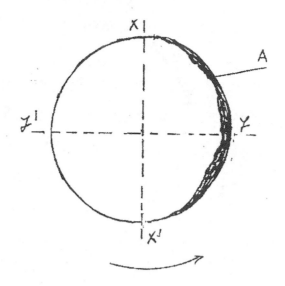

The phase with irregular edge of the Moon.
A. Irregular edge.

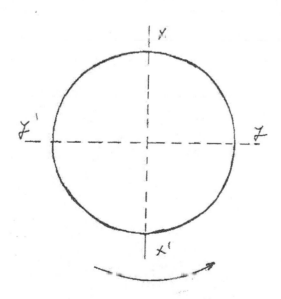

Fully enlightened side of the Moon.

According to this solution, the Moon has irregular shape, and its only one round surface emits the light. Moon's irregular interior does not emit any light that can be visible to us. This is an idea that the Moon is missing part of its body. The other existing part emits energy that is visible for us.

The other solution is that the Moon has irregular emission of energy, but a regular shape. It means that one side of the Moon emits energy, and the other side is obscured for us.

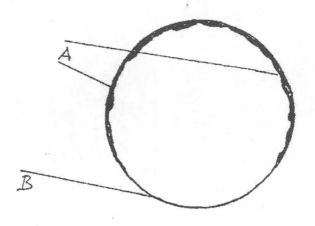

A. Contorts on the edge of the Moon. B. The entire round part of the edge.

The enlightened edge of the Moon is sometimes contorted, and irregular. Accordingly we can conclude irregularity of emission of the light. If the Moon is enlightened by the Sun energy, and if it reflects the light, than these contorts could not be seen.

In one phase the Moon is entirely round, and enlightened. The obscured side is not ideally dark, and we can observe it. Besides the enlightened hemisphere is something larger than obscured one. When the Moon is entirely dark, the enlightened edge is noticeable. The obscured side of the Moon is irregular.

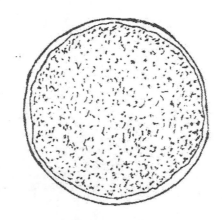

Phases of the Moon are visible during the day, when the Sun is over the horizon. A long period of time is needed that the light of the moon arrives to an observer on Earth. One such situation cannot convince us, that a phase of the Moon becomes by covering it with Earth's surface or only by an illumination of the Moon by the sun light. Such situation is denying a possibility of enlightening of the Moon by the Sun.

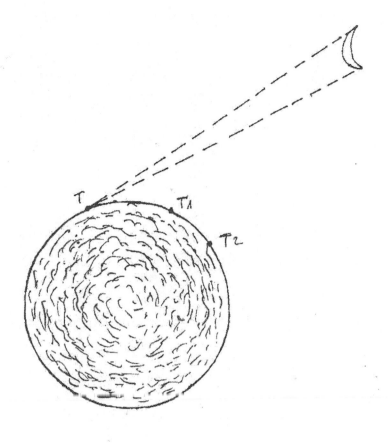

Observer in points T, T1 and T2 would see a same sight at firmament, although Earth has rotated a certain period of time. Accordingly, for forming of a phase, we cannot say that the Moon was covered by Earth.

If we see the Sun, and the Moon during the day time over the horizon, we can believe that form of the Moon is defined by enlightening of the Sun. In the points T, T' and T" appearance will be equal, although the angle of invasion of sunbeams will be various.

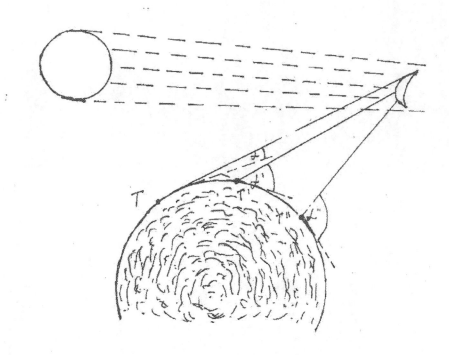

Here we can bring another idea that the Moon is the most probably occasionally covered by a black hole. Herewith, black holes are explained like hardly visible planets in a vicinity of Earth. Such planet can be covering the Moon partially, forming its phases.

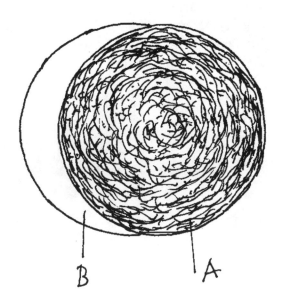

A. Black hole. B. Moon's quarter.

In this phase the Moon is covered by a black hole. This is a very possible situation. Inner edges of the Moon are ideally sharp, that show an outer edge of a black hole.

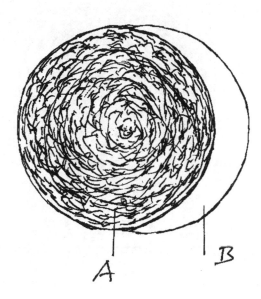

A. Black hole. B. Moon's quarter.

Same situation as above. A black hole is partially covering the Moon. The Moon's quarter is visible in the sky.

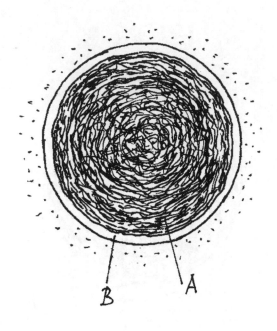

A. Black hole. B. Light edge of the Moon.

Black hole is covering the entire Moon. Its surface is a little bit smaller than the Moon's one. The light of the Moon is visible behind edges of a black hole.

The moon rises and it sets irregularly. Mainly, a rise or a set is fast, sometimes more than one hour. This matter can be explained like the Moon is closer to Earth, whose day is mainly shorter, than Sun's day.

The Moon does an emission of energy, and it rotates round its own axis, but probably slow. Besides the Moon most likely has a certain gravity.

METEORS

Earth is not an ideally still body. During its motion throughout celestial space, it meets various hovering bodies. When such body comes in the range of Earth's gravity, it will be attracted. The body will receive a power from the gravity, and it will stir in direction of Earth. On its way throughout the atmosphere it will meet resistance of air particles. The body will become red-hot due to friction with the air. Finely the body will burn in the atmosphere.

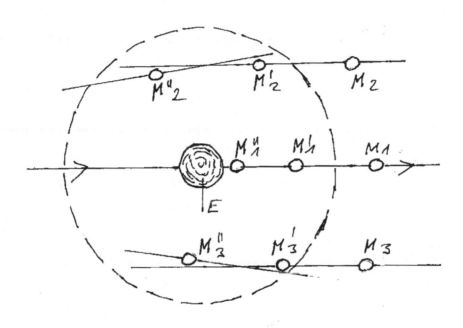

E - Earth. M 1, 2, 3 - Meteors

On the sketch above Earth is moving throughout celestial space on its path. M1 will enter into Earth's atmosphere frontally. It will be fully attracted by Earth's gravity. Meteors 2, and 3 will pass throughout Earth's atmosphere.

All depends how Earth meets a celestial body on its way throughout celestial space. It does not mean that every body will be attracted by the gravity. Some bodies will pass through the atmosphere, and exit out again on the other side. Their path may change slightly, under an influence of the gravity, but they will not fall on Earth's surface. If Earth meets bodies frontally, they may be attracted by the gravity, and fall on Earth.

This means that every body will not become meteorite, or burn out in the atmosphere. Some will pass through the air mass, and exit again. Especially those bodies that enter in the edge of atmosphere. Anyway they will become red-hot masses that transit through the atmosphere. They will be visible to us in dark nights, as meteors.

Any kind of a matter that enters into the atmosphere will be attracted by Earth's gravity until a certain grade only. A matter will be burning in the atmosphere, due to resistance, and friction with the air. The air mass around a body will be burning too. A body will form a tail from a burned air that will be visible in a night.

The question is how large the mass of a body was previously. What grade it burned to? Easily any body could have been of larger dimensions, perhaps of 1/10 of Earth's diameter, or even larger. Even thaw a body may burn completely in Earth's atmosphere.

Conclusion is that meteors enter into Earth's atmosphere. We can see the light, what means that they are red hot, reactive bodies, and they emit energy. Their masses were most probably large, otherwise if they were small, we would hardly notice them. On the way to Earth's surface, the mass of a meteor burns. Meteors reach Earth usually as stones of small dimensions, called meteorites. All found patterns of meteorites until now, were of smaller dimensions. It means that they burned down in the atmosphere on their way to Earth.

From a proportionately large body, perhaps of relatively large dimensions, it reaches only a small piece to Earth, or maybe nothing. Accordingly, we could not estimate how large an original body was. Earth is surrounded with various bodies from very small sizes, until large ones. Most probably in vicinity of Earth there are black holes of large dimensions, but we cannot see them.

Suppose Earth attracts a body of in proportionately large mass. Would a body completely burn down in the atmosphere, or it would collide with Earth. Perhaps one such encounter would derange the stability of Earth.

Meteors are bodies that do not emit any energy. They are entirely cooled masses. We cannot see them by telescopes. Mainly a light of stronger sources reaches us, as the Sun is, the Moon, or planets, and stars.

Emission of energy of only stronger sources can be transformed into the light in Earth's atmosphere. Other cooled down bodies of various dimensions are invisible for us. We cannot imagine how many of such bodies are surrounding Earth. We can expect black holes in our vicinity. We can hardly say at what angle of fall they may meet Earth. Are some of them on Earth's path?

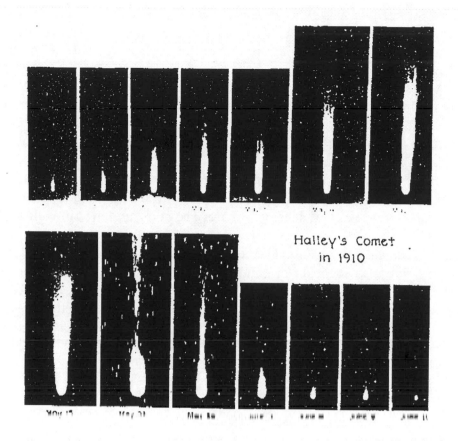

Halley's Comet in 1910

Halley's Comet

IIalley's Comet is a body alike a meteor that has entered into Earth's atmosphere and it became visible. Meteors would not become visible, if they did not transit through Earth's atmosphere. They meet resistance, and friction of the air mass, that makes them to become red-hot. The air around them is burning, showing us their tails in dark nights.

A comet is doing the same. A comet cannot become visible, if it does not pass throughout Earth's atmosphere. A comet has a tail same as meteors, which shows that a body is transiting throughout resistance of the air particles. A comet would not be visible, if it does not touch the air mass. Halley's Comet has its tail very expressed what is actually a burned air.

If we analyzed the phases of Halley's Comet in 1910, we could notice that it was only the body with small tail, when the comet had shown the first day in the sky. Day by day its body and the tail were becoming larger. In the middle of the time period, on May 15th the body and the tail were the largest. After that day the body, and the tail of the comet were becoming smaller and smaller. In the end on June 11th, the body was small, and round. The tail not nearly existed anymore.

This shows exactly how the comet has entered into the air mass of the atmosphere. It was inside for sometimes, and finally the comet exited out from the atmosphere. On the beginning the body of the comet was small, and round. The tail hardly existed. The comet just entered into the atmosphere at its edge, where the air is rare. In the same time there was not much resistance of the air mass, neither the friction. Besides the comet was far from Earth, and hardly visible.

At the second phase, the comet was already good visible. The body was larger, and the tail was already formatted. It means that the comet entered into the dense air mass. Much of the air was burning around the comet, that was hot-red. In the same time the comet was closer to Earth.

At the third phase on May 15th the body of comet was most visible. The forward edge was showing that the body was round, like any other body in celestial space. Opposite side of the body was covered with the tail. The comet was deep in the dense air mass that was burning around it, forming the glow tail behind it. The comet's glow body and the tail were most visible from Earth.

At the next phase, on May 28th the body and the tail of the comet were less expressed. The comet was moving to its exit from the atmosphere. The particles of the air mass around it were not that dense any more. The body, and the tail were still glow, and visible.

At the last phase on June 11, the comet was hardly visible. It was leaving Earth's atmosphere. Particles of the air mass around the comet were very rare. The body was still glow and visible, but the tail was hardly existing any more. Here it could be noticed, that body was round, even being very small, comparing to other celestial bodies.

A comet can fall on Earth if the gravity attracts it. It depends at which angle a comet enters into Earth's atmosphere. If an angle is sharp, and deviating from Earth's path, a comet will not fall on us. Otherwise, if Earth meets a comet under a contrary path, it can easily collide with us. A comet, the most probably, is moving in the space on a certain path with its speed. All these are elements that should be taken in consideration, how much a comet will enter inside our atmosphere.

If we observed Halley's Comet, than we could consider that it had been in our atmosphere. Most probably it was at a very edge of the air masses, where gravity had not enough power to act to the comet. This can show us that the gravity is very low at the edge of the atmosphere. The meteors or other bodies can easily pass throughout the atmosphere, without being attracted by Earth's gravity.

It is a question now, where the gravity is strong? How far from Earth surface the gravity can attract another body in the atmosphere? Even it was not sure that Halley's Comet was transiting throughout Earth's atmosphere. Most probably the comet was only hovering in celestial space, but Earth's atmosphere air masses had touched it, when Earth was stirring on her path of emerge.

Can we be sure that Earth's gravity is attracting meteors, that we see them in nights? Most probably many of them are just transiting throughout Earth's atmosphere. Some meteors will be attracted by the gravity. Some of them will fall on Earth as meteorites.

Looking at meteors in the sky we can notice that they are transiting throughout the atmosphere very fast. Suppose they were hovering bodies before the atmosphere encountered them, during moving of Earth throughout celestial space. A speed of meteors is actually the speed of Earth. Therefore we can learn how fast Earth is moving on her path throughout celestial space.

Meteors that we see during dark nights are passing throughout the sky nearby us. Otherwise we could hardly see them, as they are mostly bodies of smaller diameters. They are emitting a light energy, being red-hot masses. During transit throughout the air mass they are burning particles of the air, due to resistance, and frictions of them. Transit of a body through the air mass comes into our eyes. We can see the meteor that is passing over the sky.

A comet is a large body. Its light is much stronger, than a light of meteors. Any body when enters into the atmosphere, releases a light track, like a tail behind it. A light track is a burn down of surrounding air, and a mass of celestial body.

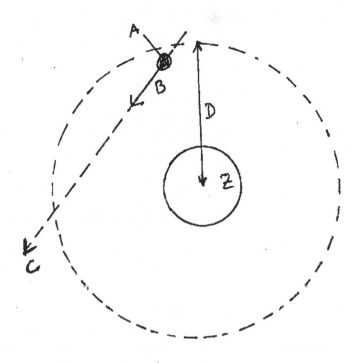

Z – Earth A – Comet B - Vector of speed. C – Direction of Comet.
D – Act of gravity.

At the sketch we can see the comet that entered Earth atmosphere. The comet will transit the atmosphere on its new path defined by the gravity, and the speed of Earth.

A comet that enters into the range of act of gravity, will receive a particular path. Suppose a comet is a hovering body. Its new path is actually a resultant of the speed of Earth, and the gravity. It means that the gravity acts even at the edge of atmosphere, influencing a new path of a body.

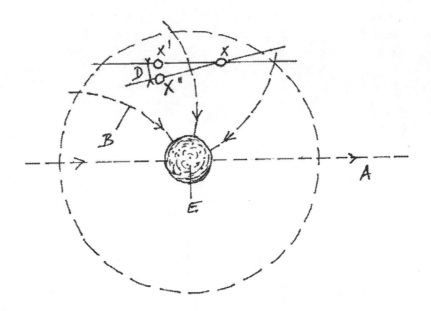

E. Earth A. Earth's path B. Vector of the gravity X. Meteor
D. Component of gravity influence.

On the sketch above Earth is moving on its path A. Meteor is in a position X. Its path is influenced by the gravity B. During movement of Earth on its path Meteor X will reach position X", instead position X'. The component D is an influence of the gravity that will attract Meteor X.

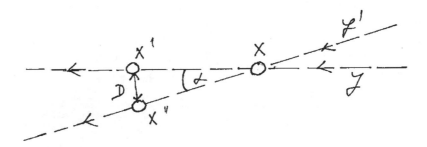

X. Meteor, Y. Vector of direction of a path. D. Component of gravity influences.
λ angle between Meteor's path Y and deviating path Y'.

On the sketch above the Meteor X is on its path Y. Due to influence of the gravity its path will deviate into Y'. The Meteor will reach position X", instead position X'. The gravity will attract the Meteor for a value of component D.

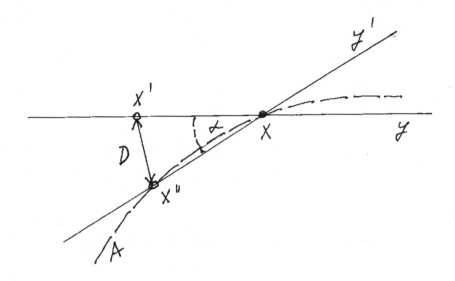

A. Realistic path of Meteor X. Y. Vector of direction of a path of Meteor X. Y' Deviating path of Meteor X. λ. Angle between Meteor's path Y and Y' D. Component of gravity influence

On the sketch above Meteor is following its realistic path A. The path is formed under an influence of the gravity. Its shape is curved and not straight like on previous sketch. Instead to point X' Meteor will reach point X" under influence of the gravity D. It will follow its realistic curved path due to attraction of the gravity.

A body is not actually stirring throughout the atmosphere at all. Its path is only imagined, being a resultant of Earth's speed and the gravity. A body will move only in a direction of Earth, for a component influenced by the gravity.

When a meteor is burning in the air mass, it is making pollution in Earth's atmosphere. Total burn of a meteor is also an argument that all matters can burn down, dependently of the temperature of burning. It means that the temperature must be so high, that certain matter burns down. Some meteors burn out totally, that no remaining of them can be found. Another ones burn down only partially, but mostly a great part of their mass will vanish. Only small remaining, as meteorites can be found afterwards.

This means that any matter can burn, dependently of heights of temperatures, and other conditions. Meteor actually is transiting the air mass that is resistant. Its mass is doing frictions with particles of the air on its way. All these conditions are necessary for burning of a matter of a meteor, such as high temperatures, resistance of the air and friction.

If we expose a matter of meteor only to high temperatures on Earth surface it will not burn out. All those components, that meteor undergoes, when transiting the air mass are necessary for burning out of it. How high temperatures meteor produces in the air mass of the atmosphere is hard to say. Most probably they are enormous high.

STRUCTURE OF BODY

If we observe what happens during a cooling down of a planet, we can find out many presumptions. We can bring certain thesis's that would change theories of nowadays physics. If a gas succumbs to a certain strong pressure, it could pass and remain in a liquid state. A component of a long period of time would be needed to lead to a procedure. In other words, if gas stays in a certain compartment, under a high pressure for a long period of time, it will transfer into a liquid state, and remain liquid. This is only a theory that can help us understand processes that happened in the nature, when Earth was cooling down

On principle every liquid passes into a gassy state. Afterwards, it is necessary to perform a pressing, or a cooling for return of a gas into its previous state. It means that a state of a matter, as liquid is, is something natural. Opposite, a liquid state of gas is something that the man has to produce. On the other hand same process could be done in the natural conditions.

Suppose that a gas or a liquid could pass into solid state under a condition of an enormous strong pressure. Techniques of nowadays could not carry out an experiment. We came close to performances that occurred in nature when Earth had been cooling down. A mass of a planet was changing its state in many different ways that could not be explained with nowadays knowledge.

The hot, liquid magma has cooled down in the natural conditions. A pressure on Earth's surface has differed from a pressure in its interior. Temperatures of cooling down has not been similar, those on a surface to ones in a depth of Earth. Besides it was also important, whether cooling down of a matter had occurred with a presence of gases, or not.

When a mass was cooling down in Earth's interior under a pressure, a certain very firm matters had become out of it, as for example diamonds. When a mass was cooling down on Earth's surface, newly emerged matters had been much softer. Such matters are the soil, sand, and surface rocks.

One of reasons for a composition of a matter is a presence of the air. Besides, on Earth's surface, there were not any high pressures, as there were under ground in Earth's interior. The air was mixed in a composition of all surface matters. That is why most of them are of soft structures. Only some rocks have a solid composition. Meanwhile in Earth's interior the hot, liquid magma was cooling in its natural form. The magma was compressed in a form under a very high pressure. Various very hard matters raised in such circumstances.

Changeability of a pressure during a formation of the mass of Earth's surface layer, that is accessible to us for investigations, has formed a diversity of matters. Accordingly all matters have become from a same origin, from the mutual hot, liquid mass. The liquid, glow magma has become solid forming diverse forms in the nature.

The hot lava has succumbed to various pressures during a formation of matters. Accordingly various natural forms have emerged. Besides pressure, a variability of temperatures of a cooling down has caused variability of newly emerged matters.

Gases have separated from a red-hot mass. They have formed Earth's atmosphere. Large quantities of gases have remained captured deep in Earth's interior. This way the natural gas has emerged.

Due to strong pressure, underground gases have changed the structure, and they have become liquids. They have remained in a liquid physical state for thousands, or millions of years. This was a way how the crude oils have become. Crude oil is a product of hot-red, liquid lava, but not of a biological origin as it is considered in the science. The physical gassy state of crude oil has changed. Crude oil has lost an ability of evaporation succumbed by enormous underground pressure, and it remained in a liquid state.

There are crude oils in various forms of thickness, and colors. Their points of vaporizations are various. There is a thick crude oil that we have to heat, to avoid hardening of it. Then there are very liquid oils, as condensates.

The gravity has kept the matter assembled, actually it has curbed it's disperse. The water also has risen from the hot red magma. Actual physical state of the water is the gassy one. The water evaporates, and converts into the steam. The vapor condensates at higher layers of the atmosphere, where it cools down on the low temperatures. Such state of the water again falls as the rain, due to an influence of the gravity.

If the water vapor does not cool down at higher layers of the atmosphere, it will remain in the gassy state. It means that the whole water from Earth's surface would evaporate, and remain in higher layers of the atmosphere. The water would remain in the gassy state forever, and it would not convert into the liquid any more. Actually the whole water from Earth surface would convert into the gassy state this way.

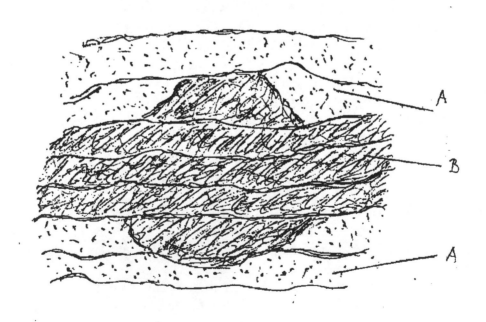

Layers of coal mixed with rocks.
A. Rocks. B Layers of coal.

Stone coal is of mineral origin. The coal also has become by cooling down of red - hot magma. Stone coal is one of variations of a variability of pressures, and temperatures deep in underground of Earth's surface.

The layers and the appearance of coal and stones are similar. On the sketch are deposits of stone coal. It means that they have become from the same hot – red magma that cooled down under different conditions of a pressure, and temperatures. That is way the layers of stones are mixed with the layers of coal, being emerged from the same origin.

Meanwhile smaller layers of surface coal could be attributed to a biological descent. The stone coal has emerged from the mutual glow matter that has been gradually cooling down in Earth's interior. Therefore, stone coal has not become from biological layers, as the science has explained.

CELESTIAL MECHANICS

The science and the philosophy have a similar base. They both have risen on the bases of the human biological substance. If we want to define unknown dimensions, we have to start from the human senses that are a product of our biological structure. This means that any science is actually made from the man. The science is only an explanation based on the human possibilities.

Until now we spoke mainly about the materiality of celestial space, respectively to solid bodies that are hovering in it. An idea of a materiality of the space could be brought. If we consider the space being material, than we have to equate it with Earth's atmosphere, actually with the air mass in it. Here, we can define the air mass, as a material medium that in celestial space does not exists. The atmosphere is material due to the air particles being in it, as one of the pettiest element of material mass on Earth. We could say, the atmosphere is vacuum, filled by air particles.

Celestial space is vacuum. It is not filled with anything, but only material bodies that are hovering in it. Therefore we can call the space as immaterial medium or full vacuum zone. Physics that will be discovered in celestial space will be different of those on Earth.

Therefore, Earth's atmosphere is a medium the most close to vacuum, actually to the space of universe. The atmosphere is actually a part of the space filled with air particles. If we presume the atmosphere, being a part of vacuum space, that is filled with the air particles, than we can say, that Earth, or any solid body is a part of vacuum space too, but filled with solid particles.

This presumption can lead us further on in discoveries of the space. We can find out that any matter, nevertheless how solid it is, is only a group of particles that are filling certain part of the space. Celestial space is immense, and immeasurable. The man will be discovering more and more depths of universe. Therefore, it could become less and less endless for humans.

The force is a product of use, or motion of a particular matter. Its own structure is immaterial, even if we can fill it over material particles. The force can express itself only in a material medium that we can recognize or feel it.

The heat, actually energy that solid bodies possess, in relation to cold universe, disappears in celestial space, and accordingly an essence of existence of a solid matter in it. It means a solid matter would disappear in the space accordingly, what will depend of a dimension of time. In other words we can say that whatever is hot in the universe, goes to equal with a coldness that is surrounded with.

We came to two essential conceptions of celestial space. It is immaterial and cold. A solid body is a hot object that is opposite to the cold space. Any heat will disappear in a coldness of the space. These are two basic characteristics of celestial space, and future mechanics that will be used in it.

Cold celestial space actually tends to convert any heat into a coldness of it. Any solid body is a composition of a heat. In other worlds being material means being hot. Any solid matter is material, and hot in same time. Therefore, the cold space tends to convert a solid mater into a coldness of vacuum.

Sun energy could be defined as being material. The material particle of sun mass transits celestial space. It will arrive and touch Earth's atmosphere on the end of its way. Sun energy, as a force is immaterial. Bearers of conception of a matter are material particles of sun surface. How small, and how much material such particles are, we can only propose.

Electromagnetic waves transit Earth's atmosphere, spreading further on in celestial space. The air mass is a medium of transmission of electromagnetic force inside Earth's atmosphere. A material particle of the air mass is a material bearer of electromagnetic waves that will transit further on through celestial space.

Meaning of a material particle is its material form, relatively to vacuum space. It is a tiny part of the matter that still carries its characteristics, as firmness, and the heat. A material particle can be compared with a projectile, and it confirms the theory of transit of a body throughout vacuum.

If we analyze the airless space, actually vacuum, we can find out, that it is extremely cold for our senses. A temperature of coldness of the space is for us immeasurable.

Earth, planets and all solid bodies in celestial space, are constructive parts of it. Collision or explosion of a body is only one of presumptions, but maybe we can talk about births of new bodies too.

If we suppose celestial space being immaterial, than only solid in it are bodies, that have emerged from a common mass. Endless of the space is acceptable for us, as an airless element, and material bodies, that are hovering in it. These are two extremities that our knowledge contains.

We can analyze further on in celestial space, and we can ask: What became first, the space, or a solid matter in it. Has the matter risen from the space, or opposite? These are two basic identifications. The space being endless, what means not entirely identified for us, and a matter as a solid structure in it. Is there any connection between these two notions?

Material forms exist in non material space as celestial bodies. Besides, meteors of various dimensions until the tiniest forms exist in the space. Is there any connection between these two expressions, material, and non material elements in the space?

Suppose that solid bodies emerged from non material space. In this case we cannot consider celestial space being non material. We can consider the space being cold, according to our biological structure, as we can feel it being so. Let's say that the space is endless cold, as we cannot assume so much low temperatures.

We can consider celestial space being immaterial, respectively that there are particles, which for our notion are endless tiny and very distant one from another. We can compare this idea with the air in Earth's atmosphere. Among particles of the air, that are very distant one from another, there is a vacuum. Same is in the space, among particles is vacuum. Only particles, or a group of particles, are very distant one from another. We can easily speak about distances of miles, or thousand of miles. Actually, a composition is the same, but only distances of particles are different.

We came to the conclusion, that the composition of air mass in Earth atmosphere, and non material space is actually similar. In the other words non material space is everywhere. It is spreading throughout bodies of various densities, or endless distant emptiness of celestial space.

A reactive force, that has separated a body from its primary planet, drives a body throughout celestial space. Rotation force, whose product is the gravity, originated from a same reactive force. This is only known force in the space, primary reactive force, and its vectors, rotation, and gravity. These are bases of celestial mechanics, actually appearance of a force in the space, and its transformations.

Another characteristic of celestial space is the coldness. We can feel on our skin the space being of such characteristic. Distancing from Earth's surface becomes colder and colder. Deeper in the space we reach, the colder will be.

Next characteristic of celestial space is darkness. A sun ray cannot produce a light in airless celestial space, as it does not meet any resistance, similar to one in Earth's atmosphere.

Coldness in the space is for our knowledge immeasurable. We can only presume such coldness, and equalize it with endless zero. A depth of darkness in celestial space is not also known to our biological senses, and today techniques.

An instrument could be made, that could be able to measure a depth of darkness. Such instrument would work with a matter sensible on changeability of the light. The unit has to be a depth of breakthrough of the light that could be measured in meters.

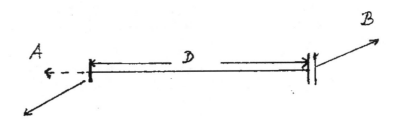

Breakthrough of the light.
A. Sensitive instrument. B. A power of source. D. Range of the light from a source.

If we ascertain that darkness is constant, than the light is something changeable. Darkness can be more, or less lightened what depends on energy of the light, that transit through it. Darkness in Earth atmosphere is different from one in celestial space. The air mass in Earth atmosphere consists of particles that are carriers of energy. Particles of the air mass, even being still and not energized by sun energy, still possess certain charges. Such charges will influence the air mass being less dark than celestial space.

Darkness of celestial space is unknown to us. Sun energy that transits the space does not show any light. Material particles being carriers of energy are passing throughout darkness of the space on their way to final ranges. Such particles are hot, but there is no any friction in the space, that a light can be shown.

Celestial space we can define by coldness, and darkness. These are only known information for us. Further parameter is a dimension of endless space, as we cannot measure it. In the future the man will be able to measure depths of the space. Universe will become more and more known to the people.

Now we have already three definitions of universe, endless space, darkness and coldness. These parameters can lead us to further investigations.

A proof that celestial space is dark is enlightened of the Earth by the Sun. Half of Earth at the opposite side to the Sun is dark. It means that entire celestial space is similar to it. The sun is a torch that enlightens darkness of Earth's atmosphere.

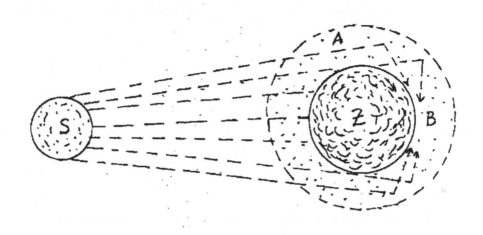

Reflected light.
S. The sun. Z. Earth. A. Atmosphere. B. Zone of reflected light.

A depth of darkness is much bigger, then we can assume. Reflected light on Earth can be seen the best in early morning, before sunrise. There is the light on horizon, although the Sun is still deep under it. Sun rays reflect on the air mass, and enlighten dark side of Earth.

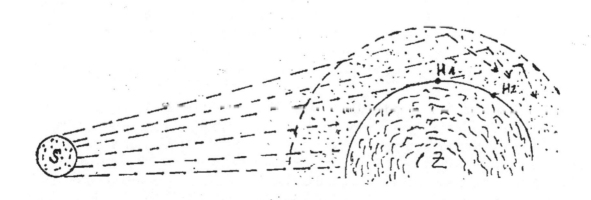

Horizon of reflected light.
S. The sun. Z. Earth. H1. Border point of a horizon. H2. Point of visibility of reflected light.

Reflected light will be seen far behind real horizon, actually at the point H2. The Sun is a torch that enlightens Earth. Other visible bodies to us can be considered as sources of the light in celestial space.

A range of sun energy is limited. Earth is in a zone of emission of sun energy. It means that sun rays can reach only a certain range in celestial space. After a border sun energy cannot pass.

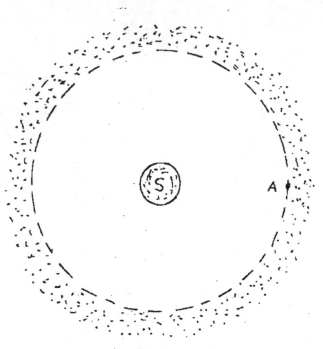

Sphere of emission of sun energy.
S. The sun. A. Point on the border of emission of sun energy.

If a body exists in the zone of sun energy emission, it will have a contact with sun rays. Heat and light can be formed only in atmosphere of a body. Earth has the atmosphere that can produce light, and heat. Sun energy that transits throughout Earth atmosphere meets air wrapping that acts as a resistor. Friction between sun energy and particles of the air mass produce light, and heat. Actually particles of the air mass become visible, and hot.

Light is actually a visibility of air particles that under influence of energy become red – hot, and visible to us. We cannot recognize the air around us, if it is not enlightened by some energy. Sun rays or electricity can produce such energy that can enlighten the air mass.

The air mass is actually a torch in this case. It is treated by energy to become red – hot, what means that it can enlighten surroundings. Red – hot air particles show us our surroundings, and the nature around us.

Earth is situated in the zone of sun energy range. Most probably the Moon is in a same zone. Other bodies probably are out of a zone. Many black holes, meteors, asteroids, and smaller bodies are in a same zone, even if they are not visible to us.

If we are situated at non enlightened side of Earth, we cannot see sun light. Sun beam that transits Earth atmosphere must directly touch our eye, so we can define it. Only sun beams that are reflected of the air mass of atmosphere we can notice.

This is a proof that celestial space is dark. Otherwise the light should be seen all over in front of us. Actually we can see only deep darkness of celestial space in front of our eyes.

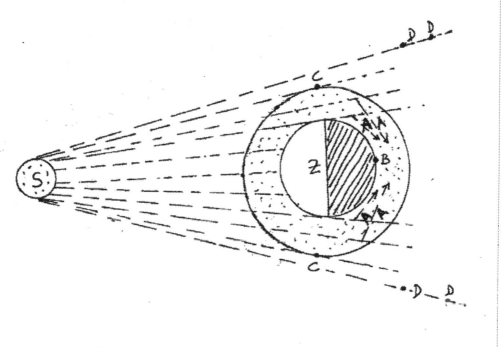

Sun energy that an observer cannot see.
S. The sun. Z. Earth. B. Point of an observer. A. Reflected ray of energy. C. Points on the border of Earth's atmosphere. D. Points at the zone of sun energy action that we do not see.

Observer at point "B" can see only reflected sun energy "A". He will not see energy that passes through the points "D", even if the points are in his horizon. Observer will see only dark space in front of him. It means that sun energy is dark, if it is outside of the atmosphere, and accordingly it is immensely cold.

Constant atomic explosions are carried out inside sun interior that is filled with the glow, liquid mass. Product of such explosions is the energy. Such energy is lanced from sun surface by a particular power. A parameter of a power determines a speed, and a range of sun energy.

All launched energy cannot reach same range. Some part of energy will reach shorter distance, than other one, that is launched under more powerful conditions. We can talk about the grades of extension of sun energy throughout celestial space.

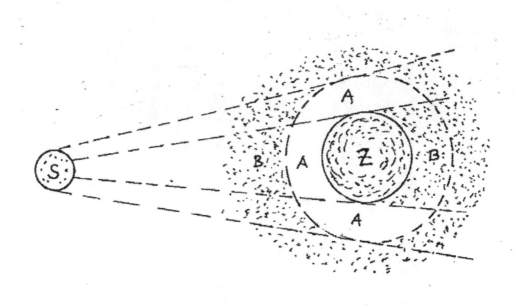

Enlightened part of Earth's atmosphere.
S. The sun. Z. Earth. A. Enlightened part of the atmosphere. B. Dark part of
the atmosphere.

A side of the atmosphere A that is facing the Sun is enlightened. Part B of
celestial space in front of enlightened atmosphere is dark. Part B on opposite side of earth
is dark. It means that entire celestial space around Earth is dark, besides part A that is
enlightened by the Sun.

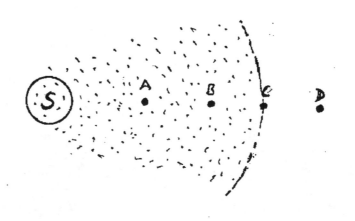

Grades of sun energy extension.
S. The sun A. Point in a sector of very strong action of energy. B. Point in a sector of average
action of energy. C. Point at extreme border of action of energy. D. Point in celestial space
where energy does not reach.

We came to a notion of transfer of energy throughout the airless space. We can accept the fact, that a body launched into celestial space, will reach a range that is dependent on launching power. A body will not encounter any resistance, as in Earth's atmosphere. We can take into consideration a transfer of energy throughout celestial space, as through non material medium under same circumstances like on Earth.

Vacuum is possible to produce on Earth, but not an ideal one. It will be dependent on the gravity. If we suck the air from a pressurized tank, inside of it will form vacuum. Some air will remain in a tank, as it is not possible to suck it all. Such vacuum can be compared with the vacuum in celestial space.

A tank with vacuum has pressurized walls, otherwise it would not be able to endure strength of vacuum. It means if we want to produce a vacuum in one compartment, it must be able to endure strength of suck of a pump that is making vacuum. Inside of a compartment, or a tank it will raise negative pressure to maybe minus one bar, or more.

Let's compare such situation with vacuum in celestial space. Vacuum in the space has not any negative pressure, like one on Earth. The airless space is a still medium that has not a physical influence to bodies that are hovering in it. On the other hand, vacuum on Earth is influenced by the gravity. The air pressure is component of the gravity that is pressurizing entire earth surface. If we want to produce vacuum, than we have to use a power that will overpower strength of air pressure.

When we make vacuum in a tank, we use a pump. Such pump will suck the air from a tank. Such tank will be closed by a valve that will secure ingress of outside air inside a tank. State of vacuum will remain in a tank that is not an ideal one. The gravity will influence even such state of vacuum, same as everything else on Earth surface.

This procedure we can compare with electricity. Suppose that electricity passes from one to another plate which is a little distant one from another. Here we can talk about non material phenomenon, as electricity transits through a non material field. Electricity will pass through vacuum space in between plates.

We can make a glassy box with ideal vacuum inside. Suppose we shoot a bullet throughout that space. We shell notice, that a bullet would pass by a speed, that it had before entrance into an airless medium. A bullet is material, and it will transfer throughout a non material space. Bullet's speed will remain the same, what means, that it will not encounter any resistance inside an airless space. Bullet's speed will decrease, only with a distance that it transfers.

In a glassy box, a resistance of the air will not act on a bullet. Its speed will not adequately decrease. Earth's gravity will not act inside airless celestial space. This proofs that a body, which enters into the airless space with a certain speed, would proceed to transit by a same speed that it had before an entrance to such space. This can be accepted for smaller distances, as a proof that bullet will be transiting an airless space, at a same speed as before.

The speed actually depends on strength of a shot. If a shot is stronger, a bullet will have more speed. It will reach a longer distance. A speed would be decreasing gradually from a position of an arm that shot a bullet till its final range. That is not only due to a resistance of the air, and the gravity, but due to a nature of shot. Normally in the airless space a bullet will reach longer distance than in the air. The reason is that it has not to endure resistance of the air, neither vectors of the gravity.

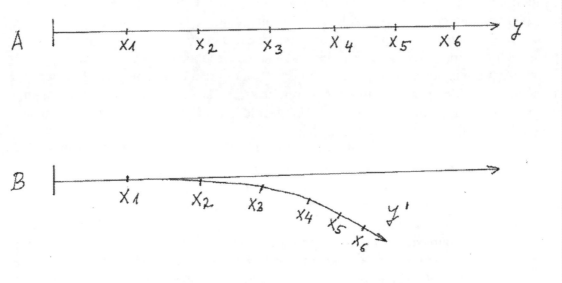

X - Graduation of a speed of bullet. Y - Path of a bullet

On the sketch A, a bullet is transiting celestial space. X1, X2 and so on are graduations of its speed that will be becoming less, and less. There is not any resistance, neither gravity in celestial space. A bullet will transit straight until it reaches its final point of range. Its speed will be slightly decreasing in a proper accordance with distance, and time.

On the sketch B, a bullet is transiting the air mass of Earth atmosphere. A bullet is not following its straight path Y, but another one Y' that is formed by influence of air resistance and gravity. Speed graduation will be improper. Fragments X1, X2, X3 will be quiet realistic, but afterwards resistance of the air will decrease its speed. Gravity will turn its path Y' in a direction of Earth's surface.

Distance, and speed of a body, that transits celestial space, will depend on launching force. A body will reach a range that is determinate by launching force. Speed of a body is also dependent of launching force. Speed will be gradually decreasing according to distance, in other words by rapprochement to its range border.

Accordingly speed and range of a certain mass depend of launching energy. A body will reach longer range, and its speed will be higher, if launching force is stronger. Here we can speak about range, and speed of energy, that will transit the airless space. Such energy in celestial space will not be decreased by resistance of the air, or gravity influence.

In non medium space, sun energy is for our notion undefined. The science accepts transfer of force throughout of material mediums, as for example, a transit of electricity throughout metal, liquid, or gas. If we examine these materials, and their thickness, we shall notice that metal is more solid, then liquid, and gas as the scarcest one. After gas we can presume vacuum, as most ideal scarce space.

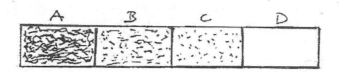

Disposition of thickness of a matter.
A. Solid matter (metal). B. Liquid. C. Gas. D. Vacuum.

On the sketch can be seen disposition of thickness of various matters that force can transfer through. Force is more efficient in the thicker matters. For example if we sway a stick, we shall notice an effect of force. A stick will be vibrating transferring force from source further on, to end of a stick. Afterwards, force will pass into the air mass near to end of a stick.

Here, a transit of force throughout a solid matter is visible. A stick is vibrating shoving an effect of force. If we sway a liquid matter with a hand, we shall make a wave. An effect of force will be slighter but still visible to us. Force will be transferring over a liquid surface showing a wave.

If we act to the air mass around us, by our hands, an effect of force will be minimal. We can feel a movement of the air pushed by our hands. Force that transits the air mass is not visible to us, but we still believe that it exists.

In all three cases same force was used, actually a strength of man's hands. An effect of force is directly proportional with a thickness of a matter. The energy will be the best utilized in a contact with solid matter, that we noticed swaying a stick with our hands. The least use of energy will be, if we act to a gassy matter, as the air mass is.

Acting with a force to the air we came close to a border of material state of a matter. Gasses and the air are last components of material state of a matter. Next component is vacuum or an immaterial medium. Force will have the least effect in a vacuum state. This means that force cannot act in vacuum, what means in celestial space. But how sun energy transit such immaterial space than?

This theme touches immaterial zone, actually it searches ways for explanations. If we want to study celestial space, knowledge of immaterial zone is important. A launched object will transfer immaterial or airless zone. Sun energy will transfer same zone, what the light, and the warmth proof, and that we receive on Earth.

Transfer of energy throughout celestial space can be considered as non medial. Accordingly, energy from the Sun to Earth transits by immaterial medium. An emission of sun energy can be considered as a power similar to electrical energy. Electrical energy transits through lead using particles of metal as carriers of energy.

During an emission of sun energy, material particles of sun's surface will be launched into celestial space. They become carriers of transit of newly raised force, actually sun energy. The energy of explosions of particles of the liquid, glow mass is transferring from sun's surface into celestial space by a material particle of sun surface. Such particle is reactive, actually charged by the energy.

How much material the reactive particle of sun surface is? Such particle is so much material, that it can be driven throughout celestial space by launched energy. The reactive particle carries launched energy of a body that it has been launched from, for example from the Sun.

The reactive particle of sun energy transits celestial space based on launched energy, and it reaches Earth's atmosphere. In contact with the air mass it produces light, and warmth. The material, reactive particle of sun surface, that transited celestial space, touched the air mass of Earth atmosphere. Further on sun energy transfers by particles of the air.

The Sun is relatively to Earth, the biggest source of energy. It possesses a solid wrap that holds inner liquid glow mass assembled. The sun spots proof existence of a solid wrap at sun's surface. The emission of energy occurs from interior of the body. Material, reactive particles form on sun's surface. They are an integral part of the mass of body.

Launching of material particle into celestial space is a product of force emerged in interior of the Sun. A material particle of sun surface will transit celestial space. Such particle will reach Earth's atmosphere, where it will express as sun energy.

We can make a box of two metal plates. In between the plates we have to produce a vacuum. If we heat one plate, and we measure temperature on the other one, we shall find out that it heats too. A material, reactive particle transfers throughout vacuum, as a transitive medial element, and it shows on the other plate of the device.

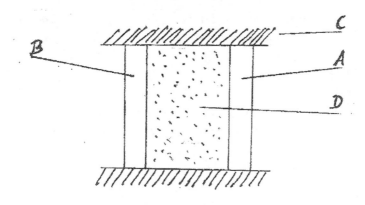

Transfer of particle throughout vacuum.
A. Plate that is heated. B. Plate at which we measure temperature.
B. Insulator. D. Vacuum space.

Accordingly, electricity as a force transits throughout non medial space. If we transfer electricity throughout a vacuum pipe, from one plate to another, it will be measured on an opposite plate. This method will demonstrate a phenomenon of launching energy throughout celestial space.

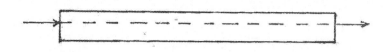

Transfer of electricity throughout a vacuum pipe.

Electricity launched throughout a vacuum pipe will have power that is defined by a source. Material particles will transfer a vacuum space according to direction, and range of launching. Electromagnetic waves that are a product of electricity transfers non medial, airless space. This is one of examples how material particle could transfer a vacuum space. This experiment may serve to us to understand transfer of reactive particle in celestial space.

Reactivity of material particle depends on a surface of celestial body. Every matter will not have same launching effect. If a body has an atmosphere like Earth, than reactivity of material particle will form in it. Otherwise reactivity of material particle will form on a solid surface of celestial body, if it can emit energy.

Now we came to a question whether Earth does an emission of energy. Earth most probably could be doing a certain weak emission of energy into celestial space. A body that posses a glow, liquid interior can emit its energy. Earth's wrap is very solid that hardly much emission can pass throughout of it.

We can suppose that some Earth's energy transits throughout the atmosphere into celestial space. How strong such energy is, we cannot say. How far beams of such energy can reach we cannot answer.

Is Earth visible from other bodies in celestial space? It is hard to answer such question. Most probably Earth emits some weak energy. If we fly over dark side of Earth we shall hardly see its surface. Actually we fly through the air mass. We cannot say what we could see, if we would be on a surface of another body that has an atmosphere like ours. Most probably Earth is black hole, like other hardly visible bodies in its vicinity.

Reactivity of a material particle is created by an influence of energy emitted from interior of a body. Transfer of energy to a surface of same body, occurs on the bases of reaction of hot – red liquid mass in its interior. Reactivity of material particles of surface layer increases. They spread into celestial space like projectiles.

Remaining of vapors from solid bodies definitely remains in celestial space, same as anything else. For example, tiny parts of solid matter that brake away from a body will remain in the space too. The masses of particles of vapors are immense small. They confront to cold surrounding, that will cool them, and equal with it.

If particles of gas are assembled in celestial space, they will do conflict on the bases of heat, and reactivity, that they possess. Any particle will pass a distance, according to its possession of reactivity. They will collide to each other, as they are moving across ways of each other. Finely, each particle will reach its own range that depends only on a reactive energy that it possesses.

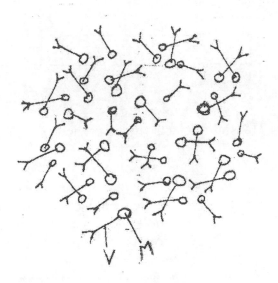

Conflict of particles of gas in celestial space.
V. Vector of particle's reactive force. M. Mass of particle.

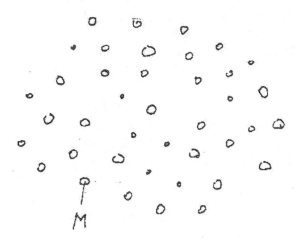

Final position of particles in celestial space.
M. Mass of particle.

A particle possesses only a mass "M". It does not possess any vector of a reactive power. A particle remains still in the space, without doing any motions. This conception is only theoretical, but particles are actually imagined parts of a matter. How tiny they can be in celestial space is hard to imagine. They tend to minimize, and become a part of the airless, vacuum space.

On Earth we can feel a heat, because particles of the air mass are bombing us. They confront to our skin being reactive and hot, actually filled with charges of sun energy. Opposite is coldness, actually a lack of reaction of air particles in our surrounding.

We can consider celestial space as a cold zone. There is not any reaction of material particles in it. If there are particles in it, than the distance between them is immense big for our opinion. They could not cause any reaction that we would feel. They are cold and minimized, actually equaled with vacuum surrounding.

In these words celestial space has some similarities like a composition of the air mass in Earth atmosphere. This serves only for our orientation in view to understand the airless, vacuum space. Solid bodies are hovering in the space. Many small asteroids and various solid elements are hovering there.

We only have to investigate, and measure celestial space in view to understand it. By and by, we can discover more, and more of the space. Celestial space will be endless for us for a long, as we shall hardly be able to reach all parts of it.

In higher layers of Earth's atmosphere, it is cold, because the air is scarce. Accordingly a conflict between particles is weaker. On earth's surface the air mass is thicker, and its particles are squeezed. They have larger masses, and they will produce a reaction easier.

If we take celestial space in consideration, than we can say that coldness is natural. Celestial space is immense cold for our opinion. Opposite, the heat is product of something, as for example product of friction, during transfer of power throughout a resistant matter.

If we heat a solid matter, it will gradually pass into a gassy state. Every matter has tendencies to pass into a gassy state. Any matter gradually divides into tiny particles of gas. Actually a matter tends to an endless division. This is, of course, dependent of a heat. If there is no heat, these processes would occur slowly.

Any matter, as being material is in the other words hot. A matter and a heat are directly proportional. Accordingly, if there is no heat, the matter would not exist.

A matter tends to split into pieces, and convert into a gassy state. It tends to endless splitting, regarding reactive fillings of its particles that produce a heat. It means that a final state of particles of any matter is a gassy one.

A matter is exposed to heat, only because it is situated on Earth, and it absorbs heat from its surrounding. A particle absorbs heat that increases its reactive energy. Heat will increase a mass of particle, converting it into a gassy state. A particle will start to confront to other particles of its surrounding. Finally, a conflict of particles and an explosion will occur.

The Sun enlightens Earth, and heats it in the same time. Matters on Earth partially absorb heat that is received from the Sun. It means that a soil and stones will absorb heat of sun energy. They will succeed to hold the energy for some period of time inside their composition.

The mass in interior of Earth is hot-red, and liquid. The surface solid wrap is an insulator that disables heat from interior of Earth to spread on its surface. The heat from Earth's interior is not sufficient to heat Earth's surface. Accordingly, we consider that, only sun energy heats us.

A solid body reaches a point of its range. If it does not possess any more a driving energy, will remain hovering in celestial space. A body still possesses cohesive force produced by its gravity that express as a strength of matter. Such strength will keep its matter assembled. A body is hot even if it does not possess any glow liquid mass inside. Any body being solid is hot in the same time.

Particles of any solid body are reactive. They are in conflict between themselves. Any body tends to convert into gassy state and equal with surrounding cold space. Still cohesive force of a body is strong. Its particles are assembled inside its structure. Particles at brim of a body will convert easily into a gassy state, and detach from main mass. They will mix with the airless composition of celestial space.

Celestial space is a medium, that does not posses any material elements, neither any defined force, nor energy. This includes only vacuum of the space, but not solid masses that are hovering in it. A solid body is holder of heat, actually of energy. On contrary universe is opposite to this notion. We can identify universe as being cold, because we can feel it being so.

Earth is hot, in the relation to universe that is cold. Earth's solid matter confronts to a very cold space of universe. A matter is product of cooling down of glow magma. Cooling down of Earth mass can be considered as long or endless period of time. Accordingly a matter, in relation to the space of universe, considers being relatively hot.

Influence of coldness acts to a solid body in the airless space. As a body's composition is a solid mass, space cannot destroy it at once. It will take a long process of erosion that will affect a body. This assumes for a body that have not its gravity. Otherwise such body will be able to hold its particles assembled and behave similar to Earth. They will become covered by ice, if they have air atmosphere.

Icy areas on Earth prove the coldness of universe. It occurs a vaporization of gasses on other solid bodies in celestial space, due to their glow, liquid mass in their interiors. Most of bodies are of same composition as Earth. We can easily expect the water and the air on the other bodies in universe.

Gases that evaporate from solid body into the space of universe will confront coldness. Water evaporation from a planet will form permanent icy wrap around it, if body has gravity. If a body has no gravity, it will not be able to maintain an atmosphere around it. A solid matter of a body will confront directly to coldness of the space. How a body will endure such contact with coldness is hard to say.

If a body in celestial space has atmosphere, it will have a similar characteristics, as Earth. It means, a body will have gravity to keep evaporated gases assembled over its surface. Of course this depends, whether a body is enlightened by the Sun, or by another source of energy in the space. Otherwise it will be only dark, and cold on its surface, that would be covered by a permanent ice.

Similarly our Earth would be covered by an icy wrap, if there was no sun energy. All water on Earth would be frozen over oceans, and other land areas. How low temperatures would be on Earth's surface is hard to say. Most probably temperatures would be mega zero.

Particles of a matter that are closer to Earth's surface have more weight, than those that are on the edge of atmosphere.

Let's take in consideration the formula of weight: $T = M \times G$

T = Weight M = Mass G = Gravity

Herewith it is noticeable, that weight depends on a mass. A mass is actually structure of a body that is multiplied by gravity. This proves that matter will weight unequal from Earth surface to an edge of the atmosphere, dependently of the force of gravity. The force of gravity differs from Earth surface to an edge of the atmosphere, actually to an edge of gravity zone. The most heavy a mass will be on Earth's surface, and the least on an edge of gravity zone. Further more in the space of universe a body will not have any weight.

This conclusion wants to prove that the force of gravity has not same strength from Earth's surface until the edge of atmosphere, and further on. Strength of the gravity could be measurable by adequate instruments.

Any matter, regardless how solid it is, will have empty, or vacuum spaces among its particles. Firmness, and weight of a matter depends on softness, or thickness of particles, or in the other words, how big is a vacuum space between particles of a certain matter.

Gravity holds Earth's atmosphere assembled. Without regard how tiny a particle is, it succumbs to influence of gravity. Whatever particles are smaller, influence of gravity is weaker. In other words, whatever vacuum between particles is bigger; influence of gravity is weaker.

Action of gravity diminishes relatively to distance of a particle from Earth. A vector of distance of a particle from Earth is proportional to an action of gravity. If particles split up to very tiny proportions that gravity cannot act on them they will remain to hover on the edge of atmosphere.

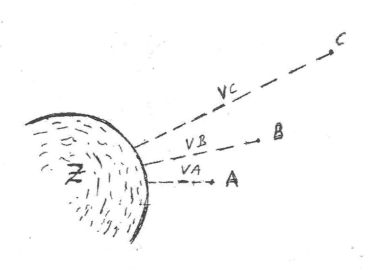

Z. Earth A. Particle in vicinity of Earth. VA. Vector of action of gravity.
B. Particle inside Earth's atmosphere. VB. Vector of action of gravity
C. Particle on the edge of Earth's atmosphere. VC. Vector of gravity action.

Particles are reactive, actually they do a movement due to reaction. Particles of higher speed reach more range, and they distant from Earth. Motion of particles and their speed are usually products of heat and evaporation.

Particles on an edge of the atmosphere on principal are hovering, independently of influence of gravity. State like that we can call equilibrium. Whether a particle will reach further into celestial space, depends on its reactivity.

On principle, a matter in the space of universe is free from influence of gravity. Particles being in such medium tend to split up, and divide. A reason is energetic filling of particles that act one to another inside cohesive structure. A final result is strewing of a matter into the space of universe.

This act practically can be considered like a loose of a matter. It disappears in the space that is opposite to cohesive force of atmosphere which is a product of gravity. In this discussion celestial space can be considered as non energetic, as it does not possess any energy.

TRANSFORMATION OF MATTER

Reaction of the flame means combustion of burning matter together with the air. The fire transfers by the air mass as medium. Wind increases the fire, and it enables inflow of the air to the flame. This means that the air is burning together with a flammable matter, as for example with the wood.

Actually the air is burning on high temperatures. The air does not only support burning, but it is really burning. This can be proof by the flame that freely spreads through the air mass. The wind spreads the flame, and it increases its volume.

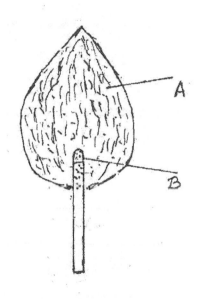

Ignited match.
A. Burning of the air. B. Flammable matter.

The flame proofs burning of the air. We can observe an ignited match, or any other flammable matter. We shall see a flame that spreads around a flammable matter. Here we can separate the air from a flammable matter. Flammable matters are usually red-hot, and glow. A flame spreads around it, what means that a surrounding air burns.

The air acts as a burning matter. It is explosive, and burnable. It means that in a fire, only the air is burning. A flammable matter serves to ignite the air, as a burning matter. A flammable matter will keep the air burning. In same time, a flammable matter will be used. It means that for a certain quantity of flammable matter, we can burn a certain volume of the air.

Now we have comparison between a flammable matter, and the air. We can make calculations accordingly. We can say that for so much quantity of certain flammable matter, we can burn such volume of the air. It would be very easy to raise calculations that will calculate quantity of the air that would be burned, for a certain quantity of flammable matter, like gasoline etc.

153

In the burning mixture in a motor, it occurs a burning of the air. Gasoline as flammable matter is mixed with the air. It will ignite the air, and keep it burning. In the same time, gasoline, as a flammable matter will be used. In exhaust gases we can find only carbon monoxide, and other similar gases, but not remaining of the air. This could prove that the air in cylinders of a motor has burned away, together with gasoline, as a flammable matter.

In the motor, the air together with a flammable matter serves as a carrier of expansion and work. This proves that the air could be used as a fuel under certain circumstances. Temperature of inflammation should be higher and constant.

On principle, all the matters are burnable, but not only the carbon. A meteor that enters into Earth's atmosphere burns entirely. It means that minerals burn on high temperatures. Sometimes smaller remaining of meteor, called meteorite, whose structure is mineral, drops on Earth.

Reaction of burning is a product of heat. A heat expresses by increase of reactive fillings of particles of a matter. Particles of solid or liquid matter assume a form similar to a gassy one. It means that particles are charged by energy.

When a flammable matter is burning, its particles are transforming from solid into a gassy state. This is example for wood, or coal that has been solid previously. They will transform into gassy state during a process of burning. Actually such flammable matter will burn the air mass in its surrounding. Same matter will be used, and its particles will transfer into gas.

Burning is one example of transfer of solid matter into a gas. It means that certain solid matter like coke has its structure. Its particles are cohesive, and assembled in a certain volume of matter. Coal is on certain low temperature, and its particles are still solid. If we increase temperature to coke, its particles will become reactive. A process of confusion between them will arise. The particles will tend to convert into a gassy state. Volume of vacuum between particles of a matter will rise.

Volume of vacuum is the reason of conversion of particles from solid to gassy state. Volume of vacuum between particles will arise, if matter converts from one state to another. If we heat water, it will convert into a vapor, or gassy state. Volume of vacuum between particles in new state of water will rise.

The more volume of vacuum between particles of a matter is, the softer, or gassy a matter is. This is the only parameter that converts matters from their solid or liquid state into a gassy one. It means that particles of such matter are distant one from another. We can bring another theses, and say, that the more distant the particles one from other are, a matter will be gassier one.

This means that all gases are not similarly dense. Density of gas depends how distant its particles are one from another. In other words, what a volume of vacuum of one cm3 of gas is? The gasses are actually compressed. Distances between their particles depend on machineries that compressed such gas. Otherwise, if gas is not compressed, its particles would disperse, and mix with the surrounding air.

This thesis leads us to another field, where we can compare water with gas. Water is actually assembled gas, what means that particles of gassy state of water are assembled into a liquid state. Water will vaporize due to heat and its particles will convert into vapor, or its gassy state. Then, under threat of coldness, such vapor will convert into water again. This occurs in the nature, where water vaporizes, and falls back on Earth's surface as the rain.

Now we can study a heat of the coal again. Particles of coal are assembled into a solid state of a matter. If we heat coal, its particles will absorb the heat that will tend them to start moving inside a solid matter. Particles will tend to convert into a gassy state, what means to increase volume between them. If a body absorbs the heat it must store it somewhere. Absorbing the heat means absorbing energy. Such energy will act to particles of a matter, making them to move, and produce confusion. Particles will be colliding each other being charged by energy of the heat. Energy actually transfers from one particle to another. Particles are carriers of spread of energy, and holders of it in same time. Particles being confused more, and more will tend to convert into a gassy state, building bigger and bigger volumes of vacuum between themselves. Finely a gas will be extracted from the coal.

Similar procedure will occur if we burn a matter of coal. Particles of coal will react with the air, and convert into a gassy state very fast. New gassy matter will arise, so called an exhaust gas. A solid matter of coal is converted into a gassy state in reaction with the air.

Structure of coal, as a solid matter is fluffy. It means that composition of one stone of coke is not similarly solid. Some parts are harder, than another that are softer. Being softer means that such part of a matter is closer to gassy state, than another one. Being soft means that already some particles of gas are mixed with solid ones. This means that such stone of coal alrcady has some gas inside its composition.

If we ignite such stone of coke, gassy parts will commence to react with the air. During burning process, solid parts will be converting into gassy state. Strong reaction with the air will influence a solid structure of coal to convert into gas, and burn out.

This means that we can ignite only a gas. Actually we can bring any gassy state of a matter into reaction with the air. In all these cases, coal is only flammable matter that makes the air burn. We succeed to extract gas from coal, and burn it together with the air. This is normally happening during burning process. It means, if we hcat, or burn coal, its gas will arise, and burn with the air. We actually burn only the gas that we can extract from a solid composition of coal.

After burning of coal some solid matter will remain so called ashes. Such remaining shows us, that we did not succeed to extract a gas from ashes. If we had better burning device, maybe we would succeed to convert whole stone of coal into a gas, and burn it out Afterwards, no remaining would be found after such burning process.

This means that process of burning is actually process of converting a solid matter into gas. In other words, we are extracting gas from a solid matter, and we are burning it in mixture with the air. This is a base of any burning process, whatever matter is in furnace, whether solid, liquid, or gassy one. Actually, it will burn only a final, clean extract of gas. It means that we cannot bring directly in contact a flammable matter and the air, and have a fire. The gas has to be extracted from a flammable matter, and mixed with the air. No matter how we shall make it, it is the only way how we can ignite a flammable matter.

What will happen with a matter that is more solid than a coal if we expose it to the heat? We can study a piece of stone for example. If stone is exposed to a burning at high temperatures for a long time, it will become white. Earlier people used such practice of burning stones that used to become white like a chalk. Such chalk has been used to make a white color for painting of houses. The stone that has been burned for a long time has become white, and fluffy. It means that gas was extracted from it. Remaining can be explained like a certain kind of ashes.

A matter consists of particles that have certain filling, what is dependent of structure of a body, and the heat. A matter has actually a particular temperature, like a temperature of its surroundings. Such temperature determines a filling of particles. A filling actually means that particles are partly converted in a gassy state, if it considers a solid matter. Such filling of particles of a solid matter can be compared to liquid or gassy one.

Particles of any matter have a particular filling, what depends on a temperature of matter. A filling means transformation of a particle from solid into gassy state. If the gas is in consideration, than filling of a particle means, that existing gas tends to build more volume of vacuum in between its particles. Any particle of the gas can have a filling that will convert it to gassier state, than existing one. It means that density of the gas will decrease, if we charge its particles with higher fillings.

This is actually only a theory, because the gas is usually compressed in tanks. If we heat such tank, particles of the gas will receive higher fillings, and they will tend to expand to a larger volume. A pressure on a tank walls will increase.

Increasing temperature to any matter, fillings of its particles will raise gradually. A volume of matter will rise. The process of an extraction of the gas will increase. A matter will be more flammable for our condition of burning, then before of an increase of temperature. It means that we still have not succeeded to bring some matters into a condition for burning.

Accordingly, if we raise temperature to any matter, it will release more gas, then before. It means that fillings of its particles will rise. The process of conversion of a particle into a gassy state will increase. Burning conditions are higher than earlier, when temperature of a matter was less.

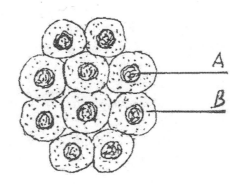

Sketch A. Particles of a still matter.
A. Particle. B. Expansive filling of a particle.

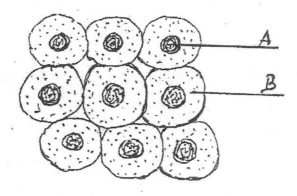

Sketch B. Particles of a heated matter
A. Particle B. Filling

At the sketch A., can be seen a particle of a still matter. It possesses particular dimensions and filling. If a matter is heated, volume of particles will increase, and accordingly their fillings. A matter has tendency to pass into a gassy state.

Same way an explosion occurs, plain one, or atomic explosion. Many matters would be able to perform atomic explosion, if they would be brought into a condition of very high temperatures, with right catalisators. Such matter would be executing tear off a matter on its basic tiny particles.

We can extract hydrogen from the water using a process of electrolyses. We can consider it being a product of refinement of the water. New product is burnable at low temperatures, differently from the water. The water by itself for our condition cannot be burned.

Carbon is chemical name for the element that we consider as main point of any burning process. It should be composed at every burnable junction. Meanwhile burn ability is not dependent of carbon. It is visible that all matters are burning under particular conditions, and temperatures.

We should approach refinement of a matter leading it to temperature of flammability with particular additives. This way we could make it burnable. Accordingly, many matters would become flammable, that would become able to be used in industry.

We came to conclusion that any matter releases the gas, being exposed to a heat, or any other extreme conditions. We saw earlier that if a steel bar is exposed to the salt water, it will convert into the gas. Only small quantity of the rust will remain after such bar. If some matters are exposed to chemicals, they will convert to gassy state.

Anyway only in the nature, if a matter is exposed to high temperatures, and rains, it will release the gas. Only strength of structure of a matter, and its cohesive forces, incorporated into building of a matter, holds it assembled. We can imagine such structures of matters like tiny framing in interior of them.

According to these ideas any matter tends to transfer into gassy state. Such process we can describe like use of a matter. It means that whole matter will transfer into the gas, and its solid or liquid state will disappear. In other words, any matter on Earth tends to transfer into a gassy state.

This way matters on Earth transfer into a gassy state in long periods of time. Such gases are filling our atmosphere, where they remain mixed with the air. Suppose that there is no gravity, the air mass would disappear into celestial space. Liquids on Earth would transfer into gassy state. They would disappear into celestial space. All solid matters would easily transfer into gassy state. Finally entire Earth would disappear into the space.

Let's study what would happen if Earth's atmosphere disappears. Sunrays would be directly hitting Earth surface. If there is not the atmosphere, it will not be any possibility of formation of light and heat around Earth's surface. Sun rays that are hitting Earth are actually cold. Entire liquid and gassy compositions would disappear into celestial space.

As there would not be the water on Earth's surface any more, the ice could not be formed. Solid matter would become fully exposed to coldness of the space. Direct contact would occur between coldness of celestial space, and matters of Earth surface, like stones, for example.

CHARACTERISTICS OF AIR MASS

Today's explanation of the air is that it consists of 21 % of oxygen. The rest is mainly carbon dioxide, and some another identified gasses in insignificant quantities, as hydrogen, argon etc. But this explanation is questionable. The air is actually compact matter that can easily become unclean by various components. It means that any smoke, or another gas can easily make our air dirty.

The instruments that serve for measuring of oxygen are calibrated to 21 %, what characterize safe atmosphere for breathing. If in the air mass in certain region traces of gasses enter, a percent will fall under 21 %, and concerned atmosphere will not be safe for breathing any more. It means that the air got unclean by traces of burned or exhausted gasses.

In this exposure the air is treated as unique matter. It will not be divided to oxygen, carbon, and other components. We can talk about compression of the air, actually regarding its conversion from gassy to liquid state. A particular quantity of liquid air will occupy enormous larger volume, when it reverts to gassy state. It means that part of the air in gassy state is vacuum. Same rule considers to all other gasses.

If we compare liquid, and gassy state of the gas, than we shall observe enormous differences of volumes between these two states. If a space that gas occupies is realistic volume of it, than the other one is volume of gas plus volume of vacuum. We can say that 1 m3 of the air consists of 90 percent of vacuum and 10 percent of the air.

Here, it is visible that in a composition of the air mass, particles are distant one from another. Between them is a field of vacuum. If we compress the air into liquid, than composition will be same, but distances between particles are much smaller.

This conception wants to express an idea of vacuum or free space between particles of any matter. The scarce the matter is, more free space will be in between its particles. This rule is the best comprehensible at gasses, that have much of free space between their particles.

The air mass can be considered as a row matter that serves for production of oxygen nitrogen etc. In this purpose there are industrial plants that treat the air due to manufacture of mentioned products. Various gasses can be extracted from the air what proves that the air is a row matter.

Mainly the air contents certain quantities of moisture in it. The percent is changeable, depending on weather conditions, and vaporizations.

Nowadays opinion that plants regenerate oxygen in the air cannot be acceptable. The plants actually breathe the air, but they exhale certain kinds of carbon compounds. Usually they exhale aromatic gases pleasant for breathing that are mixing with the air from surrounding.

Plants exhale very small quantities of exhaling gases comparing to their sizes. They cannot be compared to quantities of inhalation, and exhalation of live bodies. Accordingly the live and biological world is certain kind of pollutants.

Plants inhale very small quantities of the air comparing to alive beings that are bigger consumers. Considering that forests occupy large areas, biological world can be considered as significant consumer of the air.

We exhale non useful gas, after we use the air for breathing. Biological species exhale gases that usually are not harmful. These gases differ dependently on a sort of biological world. Some of such gases may be pleasant to us, if we inhale them. The pain wood has specific odor, that we consider being much pleasant. Exhaled gases of particular biological species can act soporific to us.

Nowadays science does not treat carbon as pollutant. Carbon is considered to be integral part of the air. Industrial installations freely exhaust carbon dioxide into the air. However, carbon dioxide is pollutant, like all other similar gases.

The technology of nowadays cannot eliminate carbon dioxide. It is being exhausted freely into the air. The air in cities and industrial zones is usually polluted by carbon dioxide, and carbon monoxide. Cars and industrial plants exhaust these gases. Stronger rules should be brought to regulate these pollutant problems. Accordingly, carbon dioxide should be permitted to be exhausted only far from populated areas. The rules should be brought, that would determine a unit of pollution, actually percent of carbon dioxide on square meter of the air mass in our surroundings.

Measuring should be carried out from a level of ground until particular height of the air that could be determinate on agreement. If results of measuring exceed certain non harmful criterions, it will be necessary to reduce frequency of traffic, actually concerned industry at a unit of surface in those areas. It means that areas of high density of CO_2 should be treated as harmful. If pollution is caused by traffic, than number of cars can be reduced. This way density of CO_2 will be reduced.

In case of industry a problem is different. Existing plants that are discharging CO_2 cannot be replaced. The only possibility is to reduce building of new plants on such area. It means that building of plants should be spread out to broader area. This way discharge of CO_2 will be spread to larger area, according to permitted unit of discharge per square meter.

Can we consider the oceans, and other waters to be generator of the air? The water as liquid mass converts into gassy state by vaporization, actually into the steam. In higher layers of atmosphere it cools, and condensates into the moisture, that returns later to the ground as a rain.

Accordingly, is there any connection between steam, or moisture and air? Is there possibility of any process that occurs between them? Will particles of steam, rain, or moisture that are mixed with particles of the air influence a regeneration of air?

There is continuous process of condensation, and vaporization. Actually it occurs due to differences of temperature of various layers of atmosphere. Evaporated water, that converts into steam will condensate again, in higher layers of atmosphere, due to much coldness there. It will return to Earth surface as a precipitation, or the moisture. That water will evaporate again with increase of temperatures. The water is in other words at permanent cycles of evaporation and condensation.

Vaporizations signify expansion of particles of the water. Particles get heated, and they assume expansive filling. Their view of an expansion manifests in vaporization, actually launching of particles on bases of energy of the heat.

If the water is heated, its surface particles will expand into the air mass. They become reactive due to the heat, and they are launched into air masses. Soon a particle of the steam looses launching energy, it will remain hovering between particles of the air. It will receive coldness of air particles in vicinity, and it will mix with them.

During vaporization particles of the air are heated by particles of the water, actually a steam. Confusion between particles of steam and particles of air will occur. They will mix in same mass, and expand to higher levels together. Soon they loose mutual reactive energy, they will remain hovering, surrounded by colder air. Their temperature will equalize with air masses in surroundings.

Particles of the water are heavier then particles of the air, according their density. Soon they will loose a heat, and accordingly, reactive fillings. They will start falling back to the ground, in forms of precipitations, as rain, moisture etc.

Expansive particles of the air under an influence of energy of heat regularly expand in higher layers of the air mass. Warmer air ascends over colder one, on the principal of reactivity. Particles of the air that are in confusion on lower levels of the atmosphere will expand to higher ones, where air particles are much stiller.

Earth gravity creates pressure of the air that acts in direction to Earth's surface. A particle of the air, that posses filling of newly accumulated energy expands in an opposite direction.

It means that there are two opposite actions of forces. One act in direction to surface of Earth, and other one acts opposite. Pressure, actually a weight of the air mass tries pressurizing warmer particles to the surface of Earth. But they, on the bases of accumulated force succeed to defeat pressure of the air, and reach higher ranges.

Expansive warm particles meet barriers of cold air. They cannot push throughout such cold mass. Particles itself become colder, and colder. They tend to equal with particles of surrounding air. Particles cool down under conditions of surrounding. They return back to Earth surface.

Expansive particles, being of evaporated water, or gas, or ones of a solid matter have same characteristics. Their reactive fillings launch them in opposite direction of air pressure action. Actually, hot particles expand in all directions, but mostly to higher levels of the air mass.

Various liquids, as fuels, chemicals etc., evaporate. Evaporated gasses rise in the atmosphere, only to a certain level high. Actual height is defined by filling of a reactive particle that will reach only a certain range, dependently on a reactive force that it possesses. Actually, such gases are lighter than the air. Soon their density equals with the air, they will remain hovering at particular level of height in the atmosphere.

Range of a particle, actually a height in the atmosphere that it will reach, depends on its filling of reactive energy. The more energy the particle absorbs, the higher in the atmosphere it will reach. Accordingly, harmful gases will not rise so high in the atmosphere. Their composition is similar to particles of a solid matter. They will revert to the ground again, linked to particles of cold air, or to precipitation.

Therefore we have salty and acidy rains, or colored rains. This conception denies today's thesis about pollution of higher layers of atmosphere.

Similarly a thesis of existence of ozone wrap is unacceptable. No gas could be able to pass throughout cold layers of the air mass. Density of any gas will equal with density of the cold air mass, and mix with it. Later such gases will fall on Earth's surface with precipitation.

In higher layers of atmosphere exists only diluted air. All dirty evaporations remain in lower layers of the air mass, as very small percentage. They will fall on the ground again, where they will cause pollution of Earth surface.

During burning occurs a production of carbon dioxide, and monoxide. Such light gases rise high in the atmosphere. They cool down, and link to precipitation. Gases again fall on the ground like pollutants. Any burning is one of higher pollutant of the air mass.

We can consider that plants are breathing the air. Actually that they use the air for being existent. Comparing to alive world, process of breathing of biological world is neglect. It means that plants will be using very small quantities of the air, we can say insignificant. It, of course depends of largeness of vegetable world. Large forests will use a great quantity of the air.

Fires of forests and industrial combustions are the biggest users of the air. During contemplation of pollution, these elements should be taken in consideration. Man has to fight against any kind of unneeded combustion.

Electricity that is the cleanest energy produces minimal burn of the air around its leads. Accordingly, it produces minimal pollution of the air. Such energy should be accepted like a most progressive one.

LANDING ON THE MOON

In celestial space the temperature is immeasurable zero, far under absolute zero. We cannot measure it by nowadays instruments. Such immense negative temperature we can call mega zero.

If biological substance comes in a contact with such low temperature, it will not be able to stand it. Nowadays metals, like aluminum etc. cannot endure such immense coldness. Construction of any space ship cannot endure contact with mega zero, neither human beings inside a vessel.

Accordingly, the landing of the men on the moon is brought under enquiry. Not any known matter can confront against an immeasurable coldness of celestial space. The Moon is most probably a body without an atmosphere, and accordingly without light, and warmth.

A reactive motor cannot work in celestial space, as there is not any air there that would serve for combustion, and drive of it. If a space ship enters into celestial space by launching energy, it will proceed to move by the same speed. Such speed will gradually decrease, dependently on launching power.

This means that a space ship after passing border of the air mass in the atmosphere will act as a body that is launched in celestial space. Space ship will reach certain range, having energy of a previous speed. It will remain hovering at point of range.

A range can be determinate by a push of space ship from the atmosphere to utmost point of its reach. Final point of range of space ship depends of strength of a push. Outside of the atmosphere a ship will not renew its energy anymore. It will behave similar to a bullet shot from a gun that has a certain range, dependently on strength of a shot.

A space ship leaves the atmosphere by certain thrust energy. A resistance of the air that does not exist in space does not affect space ship, neither Earth's gravity. The ship will proceed to move until extreme point of its range. Vessel's path will be straight, that is not a case on Earth, where a path would become parabola, due to influence of the gravity.

A space ship should have maneuverable abilities, if it has to move throughout celestial space. Maneuvering is not usable in the space. A change of path of space ship cannot be done by conventional ways, i.e. by directing exhaust jet, or by turning a wheel. Steering by one, or other way will not act in the space. Besides, it remains a question, how to return space ship, and direct it back to Earth.

Accordingly, it is impossible to maneuver in celestial space. A space ship with two reactive motors will not be able to use air jet for movement, or maneuvering. At existing air jet planes, air jet produced in motors pushes against the air mass of the atmosphere.

Jet plane uses thrust for movement throughout the air mass. A thrust cannot be achieved in celestial space that is airless. Only launching of a projectile from Earth, can be used for movement in the space. Such projectile would reach certain range, dependently on launching force. Afterwards such projectile would remain hovering in celestial space.

Any body that looses its energy in the space remains hovering in it. Such body will remain unmovable in its extreme point of range. Same rule is valid for space vessels, or projectiles, as rockets.

If a space ship has to return to Earth, it has to realize a thrust again, what is impossible in the space? A space ship would become hovering body in a point of its final range, without any maneuverable abilities. This is one more example that nowadays techniques have not reached an ability of movement in celestial space.

In addition, a space ship would be exposed to very low temperatures in the space. Nowadays materials could not bear such conditions, actually contact with immense coldness of celestial space. Metal on a shell of space ship when comes in contact with very low temperatures would suffer damages. Interior of a ship would freeze, as all biological matter inside.

In a space ship, there is not enough space for a tank of air that would serve for breathing. Such vessel should have huge tank of liquefied air. Accordingly space vessel should be of large dimensions, much larger, then one shown to us.

In celestial space a ship would collide with bodies that are freely hovering. It could not be able to avoid them, as they are everywhere around Earth. Many small bodies are hovering in vicinity one to another.

Radar is not usable outside of atmosphere. Electromagnetic waves can spread only in the air mass, where they act as a kind of electricity. If they would be emitted in celestial space, they would have different form. Such waves would not be able to reflect on bodies in the space, and return to radar like an echo.

We cannot produce push energy in the space that would serve us to return a space ship to Earth. If we would use fuel, for example atomic one, that would be able to make energy under certain conditions. It remains the question how to produce the thrust, actually the air jet.

These are the base reasons that are denying possibility of movement in celestial space. Accordingly nowadays techniques and knowledge are not enough to step over space from Earth's atmosphere to the moon, or to any other body in celestial space.

We can speak about researches in universe that are carried out only in Earth's atmosphere, or at the edge of the atmosphere. Nowadays space ships have not yet reached necessary standards, that they could be able to transit throughout celestial space.

Researches on the Moon, that are carried out can become very questionable. Any kind of space ship will not be able to transit celestial space. Here bellow is replies to the questions that have to be asked, if any kind of a space vessel has to transit celestial space.

How astronauts succeed to maneuver in the space? As we saw earlier a space ship cannot maneuver in celestial space. If it enters into the space it will continue to move by a push of previous speed until final point of range, where it will remain hovering.

How space ship succeeds to produce thrust energy in the space? Such energy cannot be produced in the space. Motors of space ship are using air jet for push inside the air mass. Such air jet is not possible to make in the space, as there is no air in it.

How astronauts breathe in the space? There is no air in space that can be brought into space ship. It means that such space ship has to have tanks of liquefied air. Such tanks would be enormously large in relation to size of a vessel. The man uses a lot of air for breathing in period of one day.

How a space ship succeeds to return to Earth? If space ship has to return to Earth it must build a thrust. It means that such vessel has to use air jet to move throughout space. There is no air in the space that such operation could be carried out.

How a space ship overwhelms coldness of mega zero in the space. Existing metals cannot overwhelm low temperature of mega zero. They can reach – 200 degrees Celsius, but temperatures lower than that they cannot endure. Space ship built from nowadays metals cannot transit celestial space.

Earth's atmosphere becomes conductor of sun energy that produces heat, and light in it. Such force overwhelms resistance of the air mass in the atmosphere. It converts air mass into warm and shiny matter.

Outside of the atmosphere sun rays are dark, and cold. Distancing from Earth's surface in space ship, we shell experience higher, and higher coldness. A difference between temperature on Earth's surface, and in higher layers of the atmosphere is substantial. Distancing far from Earth's atmosphere we shall meet coldness of mega zero.

On the surface of the Moon, and in its vicinity similar the conditions are similar. A heat cannot be formed due to a shortage of an atmosphere. A human organism could not be able to survive under such conditions.

Accordingly, landing of the man on the moon is impossible. American and Russian issues are incorrect. No one technology could endure conditions of celestial space.

Even that the Moon has an atmosphere, and accordingly a warmth, it remains a question, how to pass space between it, and Earth. That part a space ship could not be able to overpower due to low temperatures that exist in it.

If a space ship would be launched from Earth in a purpose to reach the Moon, it would use reactive energy only in lower part of Earth atmosphere, as density of the air mass is highest there. Nearby to an edge of the atmosphere density of the air mass decreases and reactive motor would act weaker. A principal of such motor is that it acts against the air mass, as against a pillow. Such principal in celestial space will not be possible to use. Besides, suck of the air in the space is not solvable. Such craft would lose all principals of a space ship, as ability to fly, and maneuver in celestial space.